MOST WANTED

Someone's been stealing designer wedding gowns and Sergeant Andie Luft stakes out San Antonio's most expensive bridal boutique. She disguises herself as a would-be bride, but the culprit escapes when Detective Bruce Benton arrives on the scene. And when he tries to arrest her, she handcuffs him and has no intention of letting him go. Bruce's fellow officers will never let him live this down, but the brawny detective really doesn't care. The lady's in charge . . . and Benton's in love . . .

JOAN REEVES

◆

MOST WANTED

Complete and Unabridged

LINFORD
Leicester

First published in the United States of America

First Linford Edition
published 2008

British Library CIP Data

Reeves, Joan
   Most wanted.—Large print ed.—
Linford romance library
   1. Police—Texas—San Antonio—Fiction
   2. Love stories
   I. Title
   813.5′4 [F]

   ISBN 978–1–84782–487–5

Published by
F. A. Thorpe (Publishing)
Anstey, Leicestershire

Set by Words & Graphics Ltd.
Anstey, Leicestershire
Printed and bound in Great Britain by
T. J. International Ltd., Padstow, Cornwall

This book is printed on acid-free paper

For two years, I've had the honor and pleasure of working with editor Hilary Sares, a consummate professional who somehow transforms a mountain of manuscript paper into eight wonderful romance novels month after month.

Thank you for your encouragement and your support, Hilary.
This one's for you!

And, as always, thanks for the memories, L.A.R.

1

Andie Luft peered through the bridal veil, searching for the slimeball photographer who had ruined her day. She only hoped she saw Lombardo before he saw her, but looking through the white tulle was like watching television — with the cable disconnected.

Exasperated, Andie grabbed handfuls of the gauzy white fabric and pulled, trying to reach the end of the length so she could fling it over her head. There must be miles of this stuff, she thought, edging along the wall quietly as she tried her best to remove the incongruously named illusion veil. Illusion? Ha. The only illusion was that a woman could see through it.

A scuttling sound to her left made her freeze. Her brain ordered even more adrenalin dumped into her

1

bloodstream. At least that's what it felt like, Andie thought, pressing her hand momentarily to her racing heart. Fight or flight? To a woman who'd grown up in a house full of men, the choice was easy.

'Come on out, Lombardo,' Andie ordered. Her fingers at last found the edge of the veil. Triumphantly, she flipped the yards of material backwards.

Silence greeted her command. The mountain of tulle caught on the tiara she wore and began to tumble forward with the momentum of a Texas river at flood stage.

Andie reached up and grabbed the tiara and yanked, pulling it, bobby pins, a few long blond hairs, and the veil free. She flung it behind her and edged forward again.

At least she could see now, she thought, as she reached into the pocket hidden in the wedding gown's voluminous skirt. 'You can't get away, you know,' Andie said cheerfully. 'So why don't you just give up?'

Andie drew the small AMT .380 from the hidden pocket and held the palm-sized gun carefully in the air as she continued inching toward the open double doors that separated the showroom of the photographer's studio from the back where Lombardo did his so-called work.

Andie reached the doorway. Still holding the gun with her right hand and trying desperately to hold the big, puffy skirt out of her way with her left, she glanced quickly at the storefront. Sunshine spilled through the plate glass windows of the empty showroom. A glance back to the workroom showed no movement. Her ears strained to catch any sound. She knew Lombardo was back there. The way he'd rolled on the floor when she'd kneed him meant it would have taken several minutes for him to recover. He was just a lot craftier than she'd thought.

*   *   *

Bruce Benton cut the engine and opened the car door. Heat blasted him as he climbed out and stretched his long frame. Summer was tough for plain-clothes cops. He yawned as he adjusted the gray sport coat he wore to conceal his shoulder holster and service revolver.

July was proving to be a real scorcher, setting new records for high temperatures and low rainfall, according to his favorite TV weather girl. During last night's broadcast, the cute redhead had even fried an egg on the sidewalk to make her point.

Afterwards, when he and the redhead had dinner, which constituted their second date and which should have ended in her bed, she'd been insulted when he'd remarked that the egg-frying was hackneyed. Bruce sighed. He was only thirty-two, but he suspected he might be getting old. The redhead, like too many of the women he'd dated lately, thought her ideas were utterly novel, when in reality they weren't even

4

a new spin on an old cliché.

Maybe he really was getting old. When the redhead had used a few choice words to describe his own intellect and stormed out of the restaurant, he hadn't even been upset to go home alone.

Bruce checked his watch. His partner had been gone twenty minutes. How long did it take a guy to order flowers? He studied the quartet of shops across the street. They catered to the kind of female he tried his best to avoid — women with matrimony on the brain.

Bruce swiped the perspiration from the bridge of his nose with his index finger and pushed his sunglasses back up. Maybe Luis couldn't decide between roses and posies, he thought, locking the car.

Heat shimmered in waves above the pavement as he dashed across the street. The photography studio, flower shop, party equipment rental store, and jewelers created one-stop shopping for women looking to drop a few grand on a pretentious wedding.

Through the glass storefront of the photography studio, Bruce saw one such woman as he passed. His hand was on the door to enter the flower shop when he stopped. Something about that woman in the studio bothered him.

Bruce casually strolled back past the studio, glancing in as if to check his reflection in the glass.

The woman looked as if she'd styled her hair with a weed whacker. Wisps of blond hair stuck up in a crazy kind of halo. Big curls hung crazily from a loose knot at the crown of her head. She turned slightly, and Bruce drew in a fast breath. That's what he'd seen in the split second as he'd passed the window. The gun in her right hand just didn't go with her wedding gown.

Just past the window, he flattened himself against the wall and drew his pistol from the shoulder holster. He craned his head around carefully and saw the blonde pivot to face the back room, gun pointed at whoever was the object of her ire.

As Bruce eased the door open, he heard her say, 'Come on. Give up! I won't ask again.'

A little bell over the door jingled as Bruce slipped through.

Damn! He gripped his gun in a shooter's stance as she whirled. Even with her gun now pointed at him, he noticed that she was a stunning woman.

'Take it easy, lady,' Bruce said. 'So you're having a bad hair day. Don't take it out on me.' He slowly moved toward her.

'What?' she asked, her voice sounding incredulous rather than angry. Her gun never wavered from his chest, but her eyes snapped to the back room.

'Or maybe the photographer took some really lousy pictures of you? Give the guy a chance. He can do them over. It's no reason to shoot him.'

'Next thing you'll say is that I'm robbing the place,' she said, amusement evident in her voice though she cast another wary glance toward the studio at the back.

'Well, maybe you are,' Bruce said. 'It's hard to imagine why a sweet thing like you would have a gun.'

'Can it,' she snapped. 'And drop your gun. Easy. Lay it on the floor.'

'I'm afraid I can't do that. You drop yours. I'm a — '

Then everything happened at once. Someone in the studio rushed her, slamming into her body with enough force to send her flying into Bruce. They went down in a tangle of arms, legs, and white satin and lace. The bell over the door jingled madly.

The woman was the first one up. She cursed a blue streak and rushed to the front door.

Bruce leaped up. 'Freeze!' Grinning, he pointed his gun at her. 'I see you lost your gun, sweet thing.'

That just made her curse more and stamp her foot like a child having a tantrum.

'Tsk, tsk,' he chided. 'Does your daddy know you talk like that?' He walked over, intending to cuff her before he did anything else.

With a snarl, the woman whirled. All Bruce saw was a white blur. All he felt was agony in his hand the instant before the gun flew out of his grip. Then a roundhouse kick to his solar plexus cut off his gasp of pain. Breath whooshed out of him as if a vacuum cleaner had been attached to his mouth. He hit the floor so hard the vibration caused a glass display shelf of cameras to topple like a house of cards. The glass shelf shattered into a thousand pieces when it hit the ceramic tile floor.

Wheezing, Bruce tried to rise.

'Oh, no,' the blonde said. 'You stay right where you are.'

Through watery eyes he saw her. She held both guns now. Both pointed at him. As he watched, she hiked up the front of the wedding dress. Though his hand felt like the very devil, and he was certain she'd cracked one of his ribs, Bruce couldn't help but admire her long legs encased in white silk stockings.

The blonde pointed to the lacy blue garter she wore on her right thigh.

Dimly, Bruce recognized a badge like the one in his coat pocket.

'I'm Sergeant Andrea Luft,' she said. 'And you're under arrest, sweet thing.'

2

Bruce shoved the folder into the file drawer and slammed it shut with enough force to disturb the everpresent pile of manila folders stacked on top of the metal cabinet. Automatically, he checked the miniature avalanche, tossing the folders haphazardly back on the disordered heap. Every muscle protested at the abrupt movement. Maybe he needed to work out a little more at the gym. He felt ancient.

If he had to listen one more time to how Luis had found him wheezing on the floor with that blond babe standing over him, he wouldn't be responsible for what he did to Ortiz, partner or not. Geez! If these guys ever found out she'd bested him with a martial arts move — he who'd had his own black belt before he entered high school — his life would be a living hell.

If he went berserk and silenced Ortiz, surely a judge would rule it justifiable homicide, he thought, considering he'd put up with this nonsense from the moment he'd walked through the door that morning. The first dozen times Luis had told the story, Bruce had laughed too. Never let it be said he couldn't laugh at his own mistakes. Besides, even he could see the humor in the situation.

The hands on the clock had crawled through a morning that seemed endless as he listened to yet another repetition of the tale. Now it was afternoon. Enough was enough.

'So I heard this crash, and I thought San Antone had been hit by its first earthquake — ' Luis began again.

'What do you think it would have measured on the Richter scale?'

Bruce leveled a sour look at Bob Scott, his so-called friend who'd asked the question.

Scott grinned back at him. 'I mean the size Benton is, the tremor might have been a record breaker.'

'I don't know,' Luis said. 'Seven point five? Maybe eight? I just know it was a hell of a crash.' Luis slapped his desktop hard to illustrate his point and knocked over a coffee mug. A few drops of inky black liquid in the bottom of the cup spattered the empty desk top, but Luis didn't stop his performance to wipe them up.

'I bet there's more than a dozen cases you jerks could work on,' Bruce said, picking up the material the FBI had faxed him about the Santiago case. 'Instead of standing around wasting the taxpayers' money while you flap your jaws about some insignificant incident, why don't you do the work you're paid to do?'

'Aw, come on, Benton. Don't take it so hard. You know what they say. The bigger they are — ' Luis snickered — 'the harder they fall!'

That witticism was met by more laughter from Bruce's other so-called friends.

'This good-lookin' babe was standing over Benton with his gun in her right hand and a Sig Sauer in her left. Both of them pointed at Benton's family jewels.' Luis grinned and shook his head. 'But the badge pinned to the garter she wore was the icing on the cake.'

Bruce's hands tightened on the papers. He'd thought more than once about that garter — and the leg it had been on. He sighed and rolled his shoulders. The movement pulled at his bruised midsection. Absently he massaged the abused area, which had been an interesting shade of purple, red, and black this morning.

He'd sport that reminder of his encounter with the lovely undercover detective from Robbery for a while. As if he needed anything to keep her in his thoughts. He didn't see a pair of legs like hers everyday. And her other assets weren't bad either.

When Luis had come charging in, she'd finally put the guns down. By then, she was laughing so hard she could hardly speak. Years from now, Bruce suspected he'd remember the sound of her laughter. He wasn't even surprised she'd haunted his dreams last night.

Just before dawn, he'd awakened, heart pounding and body ready for her. He'd realized instantly, of course, that he was the lone occupant of his bed. He was used to waking alone, but the feeling of loneliness, of wanting some-one — of wanting *her* — was new and more than a bit disturbing.

Laughter interrupted his disconcert-ing thoughts. Irritated that he'd spent more time thinking about Andrea Luft than on studying the faxes from the FBI, he tossed the pages onto his desk and rose. 'Okay, that's it! You guys have heard this same story dozens of times. Go on. Get out of here. Don't you have anything better to do with your time?'

'Nope. Not me,' Luis said.

'Me either,' Bob Scott said in unison with the others.

'I'm sure the lieutenant would be interested in knowing that,' Bruce muttered. He pointed his finger at his partner. 'Just you wait, Ortiz. Your time will come. And you know what they say about payback.'

'Hey, man, chill.' Luis grinned unrepentantly. 'It's not every day I see somebody get the best of you. Just wish I had a video of you sprawled out on the floor, gasping for air like a catfish on a riverbank.' He waved his arms and sucked in his cheeks, eyes opened wide and unblinking, garnering another round of chuckles from his audience.

'Hey, Ramsey just walked in,' Scott called. 'He hasn't heard yet. Tell him, Luis!'

Bruce groaned, flopped into his chair, and laid his head on the stack of papers on his desk. Peyton Ramsey would be worse than Luis. He looked up and braced himself for the worst as he watched Peyton approach. His friend carefully folded his designer sunglasses and placed them in the inside pocket of his well-cut linen sport jacket. He nodded at the men grouped around Luis, walked over, and slapped Bruce on the back. 'Hey, man. What's going on?'

'Not much, Peyton,' Bruce said, waiting for the axe to fall. 'What's going on with you?'

Peyton lifted one shoulder and angled his head to the side. 'Not much compared to what happened with you and Andie Luft.' White teeth gleamed against skin as dark as teak. 'Too cool for words. That just about made my day. Wish I'd been there.'

'Awww,' Bruce groaned against the background of renewed laughter. 'Not you too.' He waved his hand at the other men. 'Get lost. Peyton's already heard.' Disgusted, he picked up the faxes and pretended to focus on them, totally ignoring Peyton.

The men laughed, but, to his relief, they began to disperse.

Peyton perched on the corner of Bruce's desk and stretched out his long legs. His fingers automatically aligned the creases in his tan tropical wool trousers.

'I could have told you not to tangle with that woman.' Peyton's grin broadened. 'I know I wouldn't like to have her holding the business end of my service revolver.'

'You know her?' Bruce asked, setting aside the report.

'Yeah. She started at the substation where I was assigned before I was promoted and transferred here. I knew after one night on patrol with her that she'd either leap up the ladder or die trying. I'd heard she got her promotion. Just think, if they hadn't decentralized Robbery, she'd have been here in Main HQ. You'd have met her a lot sooner, but the end result would have been the same. I'd give a good chunk of my salary to see you two butt heads. Better than World Wrestling, any day.'

'Well, tell me how much, and maybe I can arrange it for your entertainment,' Bruce said with a lazy grin.

Peyton laughed. 'Hey, the only person in the department I can think of who comes close to her in unmitigated gall is . . . ' — his index finger pointed around the room, finally stopping at Bruce — 'you.'

'Very funny.' Bruce picked up the report, feigning interest in it as he tried to figure out a way to question Peyton without his friend realizing how intensely he was interested in Andrea Luft. 'So tell me about her, Peyton.'

'Oh, no, my friend. She's not for you. Andie isn't the type to join your harem.'

'Harem? Ha! You should talk.' Annoyed, Bruce added, 'Did I say I wanted to put the moves on her?'

'You didn't have to, my friend. I know you.'

Bruce scowled. 'I just wondered how Luft made rank so fast. She can't have been on the job that many years.'

'Hey! Andie's smart, tough, and ambitious. And it probably didn't hurt that her dad used to be a cop.'

'Ahh. So her old man still has friends

19

in the department.' Bruce kicked back in his chair, propping his feet on the desk. 'That would explain a woman like her being where she is.'

'Not so fast, my disgruntled friend. That's not what I meant. You know it takes more than favoritism in this department to get ahead. I meant she probably grew up knowing more about being a cop than most men.' He frowned. 'And what do you mean by 'a woman like her'?'

Bruce snorted. 'She looks like a Barbie doll.'

'Don't let her looks fool you.' Peyton laughed. 'I wouldn't underestimate Andie Luft. Believe me, she's no Barbie doll. And she's sweet and a hell of a lot more real than any of those girls you've been dating lately. Especially that weather girl.' He crossed one ankle over the other and readjusted his creases. 'Your problem is you don't understand a real woman — the kind that's got a lot more going for her than good looks.'

'Didn't know you were such a women's

advocate, Peyton,' Bruce gibed.

'You may joke, old buddy, but the fact remains that the closest you've ever come to someone like Andie is your sister.'

Surprised, Bruce shook his head. 'Darcy's nothing like Luft.' His sister certainly wasn't sexy like Luft. Damn! He had to stop thinking about Luft that way. The woman had beat him up. Didn't he have any pride?

He cleared his throat. 'Granted, Luft is kind of attractive — if you like that type.' Bruce thought about her long, tanned legs encased in those silk stockings. Unfortunately, that was exactly the type he liked. Or was it? Bruce frowned. This whole thing was weird. Luft was bossy, arrogant, and tough. He'd never dated anyone like that before, so how could she be right for him?

Resolutely, he pushed thoughts of her legs away. He was wrong. He had to be, he argued silently. She wasn't his type — not soft and sexy like the women he dated. The wedding gown she'd been wearing must have confused him and skewed his judgment from the beginning. Brides were soft. Yeah, that was it. He'd bet his next month's pay there wasn't an ounce of softness inside or outside of Andie Luft.

'Luft isn't in the same league as Darcy,' Bruce argued, needing to loosen the hold she had on his imagination. 'Maybe she's tough with two guns in her hands — '

'Yeah,' Peyton interrupted. His eyes twinkled. 'I wanted to ask you about that two gun part.'

Bruce cut him off as if he hadn't interrupted. 'But real toughness doesn't come from being armed and dangerous. My sister was in labor more than twenty-four hours — without drugs. That's tough.' Bruce grinned at the memory. 'I thought they were going to have to sedate her husband, though.'

'Well, I sure like Sergeant Luft's type,' Luis, who'd obviously been following the discussion, tossed in. 'Beautiful and built are my two favorite things about a woman.'

'What is this? The Andie Luft fan club?' Bruce grumbled, refusing to agree with Luis — at least openly.

'Yeah, Andie's beautiful, even if she is a blonde,' Peyton agreed. He looked wistfully across the room at the civilian employee who'd been hired a week ago.

Bruce followed his friend's gaze. 'Oh, let me guess. You prefer brunettes. Say, someone like Imena Tolliver. Tall, dark, and gorgeous. Is she your type?'

'Guilty as charged,' Peyton said, nodding and smiling when Imena suddenly looked up from her typing. She nodded in return and gave him a rather shy smile.

'And another one bites the dust,' Luis said, shaking his head. 'How do you do that, man?'

'Do what?' Peyton asked, feigning an air of innocence.

Bruce snorted. 'Like you lack for female companionship, Luis? If it weren't for you wanting to send flowers to your new girlfriend, I wouldn't have been humiliated yesterday.'

★ ★ ★

Andie parked her Miata and killed the engine. She sat for a moment even though the heat inside the small car built quickly to uncomfortable levels.

She didn't want to do this. She'd argued with her lieutenant all morning long, but it hadn't done a bit of good. If she'd known there was bad blood between Aiello and Benton, she'd never have revealed the name of the cop she'd taken down yesterday. As soon as Aiello had heard who had fouled up her attempted arrest, his eyes had glowed with a malicious fervor. She'd nearly expected him to rub his hands together like some silent film villain.

When Aiello had called her in this morning, she'd known something was up. The guy was never that friendly and nice to her. When he'd told her she was being temporarily reassigned to Main

HQ and was to work with Bruce Benton in Special Investigations to solve this case, every self-preservation instinct she possessed had screamed in warning.

The pleasure Aiello took in telling her the news made it clear to her he was dishing up a heaping serving of payback to somebody. Since she hadn't done anything to deserve that kind of treatment — at least not lately — Benton had to be the object of his desire.

Since arguing with her boss did no good, she'd spent the rest of the morning finding out everything she could about Sergeant Bruce Benton. Though he had an impressive record, she hadn't been impressed. Andie sighed. Okay, so she had been impressed — a little. A little? Okay, okay, she thought crossly. A lot.

Disgusted, she flipped the sun visor down to check her appearance in the mirror even as she chided herself for her vanity. What did it matter how she looked? She was definitely not out to dazzle Benton. From what she learned, he was the type of man she avoided — a Romeo with a bigger libido than the state of Texas. Plus he was a cop, which definitely made him off-limits.

Andie opened the car door and swung her legs to the side. She reached behind her and grabbed a pair of high-heeled sandals from the passenger seat and exchanged them for the sneakers she'd worn. She always wore heels when she went up against the big boys. Though five feet ten inches in her stocking feet, she felt the heels — and an attitude — helped give her a bit of an edge.

Slipping the strap of the handbag that held her weapon over her right shoulder, she hurried to the air-conditioned building. Even for Texas, the heat had been the topic of everyone's conversation this summer. It was the hottest July Andie could recall.

By the time she ducked inside the sprawling building that housed the main headquarters of the San Antonio

Police Department, Andie was more than a little damp with perspiration. Cold air wafted from the air-conditioning vents. Was it ever going to rain this summer, she wondered, lifting her hair off the back of her neck and letting the cold air flow over her heated skin.

With a quick glance at her wristwatch, she quickened her steps. If she could get everything settled with Vasquez and Benton, she'd be able to get home a little early and take a nap before she had to dress for her date tonight. She'd done more tossing and turning last night than sleeping. For that, she could thank Detective Benton.

Tonight would be her fourth date with Wade Pearce. A sigh escaped her. She'd had such high hopes that Wade would be The One. She smiled ruefully. She always thought of her dream man in capital letters. Wade was sweet and kind and considerate. But despite her trying her best to fall in love with the handsome accountant, Wade wasn't The One, which was too bad because he really was nice. A sigh escaped her as she neared the office for Special Investigations. Wade was, in a word, dull!

Andie considered the possibility that she might have to rethink her dating strategy. She'd grown up in a testosterone-fueled household, with a former cop for a father, and four hard-headed brothers, not to mention a nutty grandfather who made John Wayne seem tame by comparison. Nice just didn't cut it.

Andie pushed open the door to Special Investigations. She hated to admit it, but a guy like Bruce Benton made her heart flutter more than a little — certainly more than Wade or any of the other successful businessmen she'd dated.

Yesterday, when Benton had picked himself off the floor, he'd come up fighting. She couldn't imagine Wade wanting to go a round or two with a woman — even if the woman had just kicked his behind, metaphorically speaking.

Benton, though . . . Andie's eyes

seemed to zero in on him like a sharpshooter on a bull's-eye. She paused and just stood there a minute, trying to calm the emotions that swept through her when she saw him at the far end of the room. Even though his back was turned to her, she recognized him immediately. He was so different from Wade and her other boyfriends. His straight black hair appealed to her far more than Wade's blow-dried blond perfection. Benton's hair looked as if he styled it by running his fingers through it. The thought of doing the same herself did funny things to her insides.

Andie took a deep breath and started across the room. Her heart beat far more rapidly than it should. Yesterday, it had taken all her willpower to conceal the effect he had on her. She waited for him to turn and see her. She hadn't realized how much she looked forward to another encounter with him.

He had the kind of face that made women look twice. Maybe it was the hint of laughter evidenced by the faint lines at the corners of his gray eyes that said he'd be fun to play with. Or maybe it was his mouth — the sensual full lips — or the way he looked at her, as if some silent message emanated from him, a message easily picked up by female radar. It was all too clear he knew how to make a woman weak in the knees.

Andie nearly stumbled at that thought. She already felt weak in the knees. This would never do. Come on, she chided herself silently. Lock those thoughts in a closet and throw away the key.

Besides, she reminded herself, according to the gossip she'd gleaned this morning, Bruce Benton never lacked for a woman in his life. One of his former girlfriends — now married — who worked in Records had been more than happy to talk about him. Andie hadn't missed the wistfulness in her voice. Maybe women always felt pensive about the one who got away.

According to her, as soon as she'd started making matrimonial sounds, Benton had left skid marks, but first, he'd been nice enough to fix her up with one of his friends. The ex-girlfriend had ended up marrying the friend.

If ever a man had a problem making commitments, it was Benton. Yet Andie found herself sorely tempted by him. And that would never do. Besides, he had so many women on a string, he couldn't possibly make time in his crowded schedule for her. After all, the man had to sleep sometime.

3

Benton was talking and laughing with his partner Luis Ortiz and her old friend Peyton Ramsey. If Luis Ortiz hadn't walked in yesterday at the critical moment, she probably would've had to subdue Benton again, Andie thought. Not that she couldn't have handled him. Her brothers and her dad — even her grandfather — had taught her every dirty, street-fighting technique there was.

Even now that she knew Benton had a black belt in aikido, she figured she could still take him. The element of surprise was always on the side of a woman. Just like now, she reminded herself, standing a little taller, cloaking herself in attitude as if it were armor.

As she walked toward Benton, excitement rushed through her at the thought of tangling with him again.

Even his voice made her pulse flutter, she thought, listening in as he talked to his friends.

'Hey, Peyton. I'm not the cowboy here. Who waded into that quick stop hold-up last week like Clint Eastwood?' he asked.

Andie halted a few feet away. She watched Peyton flick an imaginary speck of lint from the sleeve of his exquisitely tailored tan jacket. She smiled. Peyton was always impeccably groomed.

'Eastwood?' Peyton grimaced. 'If you're going to compare me to a movie actor, try Danny Glover in *Silverado*. He packs that big Sharps rifle, you know what I'm saying?'

Benton still hadn't noticed her even though the office chatter had quieted as she'd walked through. She sensed every eye on her — and the intense curiosity that only cops seemed to have.

'Whatever,' Benton said. 'Either way, you're just as much a department rebel as I am, so don't go calling me a cowboy. If there's any cowboys in the department, your friend Luft is one.'

'You mean cowgirl,' Ortiz threw in. Benton looked up and noticed Andie in that moment. She saw his eyes widen a little, but he remained silent. His lips twitched, but he suppressed his grin.

'No, she's too tough to be called a girl anything,' Benton argued. 'She probably sprinkles testosterone on her cornflakes in the morning.'

Peyton grinned and pushed off the desk. 'I don't know. That doesn't jibe with the way I remember Andie. She was one lovely lady.'

'Well, okay, she's easy on the eyes,' Bruce admitted grudgingly.

The flutter inside her intensified. So Benton thought she was pretty. Andie immediately told herself she shouldn't be pleased. She had to quit thinking along these lines. Firmly, she reminded herself that Benton was off-limits.

'And she's still one lovely lady,' Peyton said, holding out both hands to her.

Andie walked up and took both his hands in hers and stood on tiptoe to kiss his cheek. 'Hey, big guy.'

From the corner of her eye, she saw Benton vault from his chair. 'You!'

'Yes, me,' she replied, sounding far more calm than she felt. He looked yummy, she thought, looking him over. Dressed as he was, she could really appreciate his body. Faded jeans rode low on his lean hips. An old San Antonio Spurs T-shirt clearly revealed muscular biceps beneath the thin cotton.

'What are you doing here?' Benton demanded.

'Don't mind him, Sergeant Luft,' Ortiz said, shaking her hand. 'He's been in a rotten mood since yesterday.'

Andie grinned, determined not to let anyone — especially Benton — discover the feelings that rioted through her. 'He's probably feeling a bit stiff and sore. I know that always makes me out of sorts.'

Benton scowled. Unfortunately, that

didn't make him look less handsome. Anyone else dressed like that would look like a slob, but Benton looked sexy. She was definitely in trouble.

'Shut up, Ortiz,' Benton said. 'What do you want, Luft?'

'Oh, I just wanted to see if you were okay. I didn't do any lasting damage, did I?' She looked into his gray eyes — actually more silver than gray, she realized — and nearly forgot why she'd come to HQ. Something in his eyes made a shiver race up her spine. Gut instinct told her Benton wouldn't be a boring date.

'I'm just fine. Couldn't be better. And you?' he asked.

Despite herself, Andie blushed. Benton held her gaze and made her pulse accelerate like a car thief racing away in stolen wheels. It took all her effort to smile calmly. 'I'm fine, too. But it sure is hot today, isn't it?' She fanned herself, hoping everyone thought the three-digit temperature outside was the cause of her red face.

'How's your dad?' Peyton asked.

Gratefully, she turned to Peyton Ramsey. 'Good. He's good. You should come visit sometime.'

'You're right. I should. I'll do that. Does he still have that old car he was going to restore?'

Andie laughed. 'Yes. It's still in the garage. Now and then, he'll tinker with it, but I doubt he'll ever get it finished. What about you, Peyton? Still have the same hobby?'

He looked puzzled. 'What do you mean?'

Andie giggled. 'Chasing girls. Or did Paula cure you of that?'

Peyton shrugged. 'Paula — that's over. She decided she didn't want to get serious about a cop.'

'Oh. I'm sorry.' Andie smiled ruefully. 'I can't say I blame her, though. I have the same policy. No cops.'

'What's the matter? Aren't cops good enough for you?' Benton asked, sounding more irritated than the subject warranted.

37

Andie fought the magnetic pull of his silver eyes. Annoyed that his good looks were getting to her, her voice was sharper than it should have been. 'Not that it's any of your business, Benton, but I know what a cop's life is like. Why would I want to date a guy who lives for his job?'

That was close enough to the truth. Few knew the underlying reason for her position, and she saw no reason to include the sexy detective in that number.

Defiantly, Andie planted her bottom on Benton's desk, invading his territory. She grinned and said, 'Please, gentlemen, sit.'

Peyton Ramsey and Luis Ortiz immediately dropped into their chairs.

'Yeah, just make yourself at home, Luft,' Benton said as he dropped into his chair.

'Thanks, I will.' Andie suspected he wouldn't be quite so magnanimous later.

'So if you didn't come to ask me to

the prom,' Benton said, 'what are you doing here?'

The way he looked at her put her back up. Surely he didn't think she'd come just to see him? That would never do.

'I told you — I just wanted to check on you and make sure I didn't hurt you too badly yesterday.'

Ortiz and Peyton guffawed.

Her comment was about as well-received as an order to put in eight hours of overtime. Benton's mouth stretched into a semblance of a smile. 'What? That little love tap you gave me?'

'Love tap?' Andie should have known he'd be like her brothers. They'd never admit a female could best them either. She pretended to frown. 'I must be losing my touch. I was certain I heard a rib crack.'

Benton's smile became strained. 'Anyone ever tell you you're a royal pain in the — '

'Benton!' All heads swung to Lieutenant Rafael Vasquez, who stood in the doorway of his office. 'Quit detaining Sergeant Luft and send her in here.'

Andie hopped off his desk as Bruce stood.

'Why does Vasquez want to see you?' he asked, grabbing her forearm as she stepped past him. Big mistake. Her skin felt like silk beneath his hand. He slid his fingers up a couple of inches, savoring the sensation. Desire shot like an arrow from the point of contact straight to his groin.

Her gaze dropped to where his hand held her arm, then flashed up to his eyes again. He saw the awareness in her startled green eyes. She felt it too. Good. Benton smiled, satisfied — for the moment, anyway. She didn't return his smile, but her eyes never left his. Slowly, she pulled her arm free and took a step away from him.

Bruce felt as if time slowed. He could swear he heard his heart beating as it furiously pumped blood to the part of his anatomy that demanded it.

In a voice so soft only she could hear,

he taunted, 'What's the matter, Luft? Scared?'

Without saying another word, she turned and walked briskly toward Vasquez's office.

Bruce watched her sashay away, and knew his weren't the only eyes admiring the sway of her hips in the short khaki skirt and the subtle, but sexy, curves beneath the bright red cotton top. There was no doubt in his mind that Andie Luft was pure trouble. If he was smart, he'd forget all about her. He settled himself into his chair and rolled up to his desk.

'Benton!'

Bruce sighed. For the hundredth time he wished Rafael Vasquez would learn a way to communicate other than roaring.

'Yeah?' he asked. Someone should tell Rafe that he barked like a chained dog. Of course, the guy kind of looked like a junkyard dog, too — tough enough to chew barbed wire — so maybe it was a given.

'My office, *por favor*.'

Somehow, Bruce sensed that something smelly and unpleasant was about to hit the old fan blades. He took his time and ambled in just in time to hear the lieutenant say, 'I'll tell you up front, Sergeant Luft, Benton isn't going to like this.' More than a hint of a smile creased Vasquez's bronzed features, which made Bruce instantly more wary. The lieutenant had a weird sense of humor.

'What won't I like?' he asked, gripping the back of the empty chair next to the one occupied by Andie Luft.

'You're being temporarily reassigned, *compadre*.'

'What? You can't do that, Rafe. I've been working on the Santiago case for three months.' He held his thumb and index finger a half inch apart. 'I'm this close to nailing him.'

'Unfortunately, Santiago will be around when you finish this assignment. You can nail him then. Maybe.'

Bruce turned narrowed eyes to Andie

Luft. 'This is your doing, isn't it?'

'Sergeant Luft is following orders. You should try it sometime, Benton.' Rafe pointed to the chair. 'Now sit and listen.'

'I'll stand, thanks.'

'I said sit,' Vasquez barked.

Maybe Vasquez should be in charge of the K-9 unit, Bruce thought resentfully as he obeyed. He drummed his fingers on the wooden chair arm. Just wait till he got Luft alone. How dare she waltz in here and get him reassigned with a snap of her pretty fingers? There was more she could do with those delicate fingers than complicate his life. Startled by the unexpected thought, he slouched down and clamped his mouth shut.

'If it's any comfort, I didn't much like this idea either,' she said, 'but you are the reason I lost Lombardo. So you owe me.'

He pinned her with his stormy gray eyes. 'I don't owe you a damned thing.' He turned back to Vasquez. 'Exactly what do you mean by reassigned?'

'Enough of that, Benton. Shut up and listen. Aiello wants — '

Bruce jumped up, suddenly angry. 'Aiello! I should have known that weasel was in on this.' He had several other things to say about the man, but Rafe roared for quiet before Benton could get them all out.

'I said shut up and listen.' Rafe pointed to the chair. 'Now sit!'

Sulking, Bruce obeyed. Just wait till he got his hands on that little egomaniac Aiello. His vows of vengeance ended abruptly when he heard Vasquez bark another order. 'You and Luft will work together to finish this assignment.'

'What? Work with her? Reassigned? To her?' he sputtered. This would never do. He didn't want her for a partner. At least not of the law enforcement variety. 'Begging your pardon, Lieutenant, but no way in hell! You're not sticking me with . . . with Nancy Drew! Ortiz is my partner.'

'Not this month he isn't. Ortiz still has four weeks of medical disability. Better get used to the idea, amigo.'

When Bruce opened his mouth to argue some more, Rafe held up his hand. 'Won't do you a bit of good to protest. You did bungle Luft's undercover assignment and that sawed-off runt Aiello has the clout to get what he wants. Just consider yourself well and completely screwed on this one, *compadre*.' He added hastily, 'No offense, Sergeant Luft.'

'None taken.' Andie Luft looked amused. 'Look, Benton, if you hadn't interfered, I'd have Lombardo in jail now. But you blew my cover. All I can do now is call the shots from behind the scenes and let you be my front man. Like I said, I don't like the idea either, but I can't do anything about it. Apparently, you can't either.'

'I'd rather swim the Guadalupe naked with all the tourists on the Riverwalk watching,' Bruce muttered. Somehow, he'd get out of this. Not that he had anything against women cops. He just didn't want to have one for a partner. Especially not this one. He wanted Andie Luft in his bed, not on an assignment with him.

'Can it, Benton. It's a done deal.'

'So this is the kind of support I get from my L-T.' Bruce snorted. His brain worked furiously, trying to find a way out of what promised to be an intolerable situation.

'That's enough!' Vasquez swore in Spanish, then said, 'You'll work together to close this case. All this bitching and moaning isn't going to alter that fact. Now get out of here.'

'Is she supposed to share office space here?' Bruce asked stiffly. What had he ever done to deserve this? Having Andie Luft around all day, every day, would drive him crazy.

'You two work out the details. I don't want to hear about it, and I sure don't want to hear any more whining from Aiello. Just clear the case.' Vasquez made a shooing motion at them. 'Don't let the door hit you on your way out.'

'Yes, sir.' Bruce stomped out of the room and didn't hold the door for his new partner. *Partner?* He stifled a groan.

Andie thanked the lieutenant, then opened the door and walked back to her new work area. Benton's body posture was a picture of outrage. She couldn't say she blamed him either. She wouldn't want a new partner forced on her either. Especially if the person doing the forcing was someone like Aiello. Not for the first time, she wondered what Benton had done to incur the man's hatred.

Though her sympathy was aroused, she reminded herself that it was Benton's fault she'd lost Lombardo. Still, she hated to get off on the wrong foot with him since they were going to have to work together now. 'Hey, I don't exactly want to be stuck with you either,' she said as she walked up to him. 'It took me weeks to get close to Lombardo. Why don't we bury the

47

hatchet and make the best of this situation?'

'Where do you plan to bury it? In my back?' Benton snarled, pacing restlessly around his desk.

'If necessary,' she answered, smiling sweetly. Then she added, 'For what it's worth, I didn't know you were a cop yesterday when you came charging in like the cavalry.'

'You didn't exactly give me a chance to tell you.'

'Hey, I was taught to kick first and ask questions later,' she joked. A ripple of laughter followed her remark, making her realize they had an audience. She looked around, and the other people in the office suddenly became very busy. Every cop shop was the same. Within twenty-four hours, every man and woman on all the shifts would know about this.

'So where do I sit?' she asked, looking pointedly at Benton's own chair.

'In your dreams,' he said, dropping

quickly into his swivel chair as if to prevent her from commandeering it.

A grin she could only describe as sexy creased his face.

He leaned back, propped his feet on the desk and patted his lap. 'How about here, sweet thing?'

Andie didn't dare let him realize how much he attracted her. She didn't miss a beat. 'In *your* dreams.' She arched a brow. 'Besides, I'm afraid that might be too much pressure on your bruised middle. Sweet thing.'

Luis Ortiz stood and pushed his own chair over, parking it parallel to Benton's chair. 'I'm only in for a visit today. Still on medical for a few more weeks. I can sit in the visitor's chair by my desk. Please. Use my chair and desk.' He winked and added, 'Use me.'

Andie's smile could have launched a thousand ships — and Benton's scowl could have torpedoed them before they reached open water.

'That's very kind of you, Ortiz.'

'No problem.' Ortiz smiled back at

her. 'And, please, call me Luis.'

'You're wasting those megawatts, Ortiz,' Benton snapped. His face resembled a thundercloud.

Luis frowned. 'What do you mean?'

'She doesn't date cops. Better save your charm for the nurse you sent the flowers to yesterday.'

'You're being insulting,' Andie said.

Benton shrugged. 'So?'

Luis studied his partner. 'Uh, Bruce, you feeling all right?' He turned to Andie. 'Maybe he got a concussion in that fall. I've never seen him be less than a perfect gentleman to a lady. Especially one as pretty as you.'

Andie grinned at the flattery that Luis dished out so effortlessly. All her life, people had told her how pretty she was, but in her family, achievements meant more than looks. She attached little significance to Ortiz's compliments. She'd have been more flattered if he'd admired her achievements as a police officer.

Still, Andie wondered why her new

partner wasn't living up to his reputation. 'Maybe Benton is nice only when he can get something in return. Since there's no way I'll date him, he doesn't see any need to expend the effort.'

'Hey! I don't recall asking you for a date, Luft,' he shot back.

Luis laughed. 'You could be right, Andie.'

'Luis, go home. I'm tired of you two talking about me as if I'm not here.'

Luis dismissed Bruce's demand with a laugh and a wave of his hands.

'Oh, come on, Benton. Or should I call you Bruce?' Andie gave him the same brilliant smile she'd given Luis.

'Won't work with me, cupcake,' Bruce said, clasping his hands behind his head and smirking at her. 'You'll have to do more than smile to get your way with me.'

'Cupcake?' Andie looked thoroughly irritated.

4

Satisfied that he'd ruffled her feathers, Bruce grinned. She looked so darn cute with her cheeks all red. 'Yes, cupcake. You obviously don't like being called sweet thing.' Maybe a good offense was his best defense against the desirable Sergeant Luft. For good measure he added, 'Probably because there isn't a sweet bone in your body.'

'You leave my body out of this! What's wrong with my name?' she snapped. 'Most people resort to cutesy nicknames because they can't remember a person's real name. Is that your problem?'

He ignored her question. 'Cupcake,' he repeated, nodding slowly.

'Call me Andrea. Or Andie. Even Luft,' she ordered.

Bruce acted as if he were considering her demand. 'Andrea,' he murmured.

He shook his head. 'Nope. That won't fit the parameters,' he continued, as analytical as a forensics witness testifying in court. 'Andie makes you sound like a man.' He looked her up, then down, then up again, suspecting his obvious appraisal was making her blood boil. But she refused to be intimidated. She met his gaze with defiance flashing from her green eyes. He had to admire her for that.

'You're definitely not a man,' Bruce said, throwing in a leer that would have reduced a lesser woman to physical violence. He intended to get her so mad at him she wouldn't give him the time of day. He wouldn't have to worry about keeping her at arm's length after this.

'And Luft — well, that sounds cold and unfriendly.' His silver eyes gleamed as he looked her over from her head to her toes one more time. 'We're going to be partners, and partners should never be cold,' he said softly. 'We can be as tight as any two' — he winked broadly

— 'partners have ever been.' That should do it, he thought, satisfied that he'd totally alienated her.

Andie was on to Benton now. No one could be that much of a jerk. He was trying his best to annoy her. But why? She didn't have a clue.

From what she'd heard about him, she'd have been surprised if he hadn't flirted, but the way he was acting was a parody of flirtation. She was used to handling guys who acted as if she were brainless. She blamed pop culture for the bad rep blondes had, but fighting a stereotype was like wrestling with shadows. So she'd learned early to ignore the ogling. Normally, it didn't bother her, but Bruce's gaze made her feel different. Very different.

'How do you feel about it?' Benton asked.

'About what?' Andie cringed at the breathless note in her voice. He couldn't know what she was feeling!

'About my calling you cupcake, of course.'

Her brows snapped together. She'd had all of this game she intended to take. 'Cupcake is something you'd call a cute, sweet little girl. Which I'm not,' she snapped.

'Oh, I don't know. You look absolutely delicious, just like a sweet bite of frosted cake.'

Suddenly it dawned on her that he was looking for an edge in their relationship — a way to get the upper hand. Her eyes brightened at the challenge. She'd show Benton who was in control. Let's scc how he liked being on the receiving end of this nonsense, she thought, wetting her lips with the tip of her tongue as provocatively as she could. She'd rarely tried to exploit her sex appeal, but she'd make an exception, just for him.

Andie laughed — the kind of breathless giggle that men seemed to like. She noticed Luis and several other men stop what they were doing and turn to look at her. For good measure, she ran her hands down her hips, as if smoothing wrinkles from the short skirt. She lingered over the task.

When Benton flushed, she knew she'd made an impact.

'Sergeant,' she cooed, fiddling with a button on her blouse. She lifted the material away from her, moving it rapidly up and down as if she were trying to cool off. 'My goodness,' she drawled. 'Is it hot in here or is it me?'

'I think maybe the AC's not working properly,' Benton said, brushing a lock of long black hair from his forehead.

He looked hot. Good. 'Bruce?' she asked.

'Uh, yeah?' Benton said, dragging his gaze from her shirt front.

Andie smirked. Who had the edge now? 'Since we're going to be partners, let's put aside our personal feelings and get down to business.'

'Partners?' Luis exclaimed, breaking the mood between her and Benton. 'You and Bruce?'

'Why, yes, until this case is closed,' Andie answered.

Laughter rang through the room, startling her.

'You had to go and tell everyone we were partners, didn't you?' Benton asked, sounding as disgusted as he looked.

'Did you expect to keep it a secret?' She opened her eyes wide with feigned innocence.

'Yes,' he answered, startling a real laugh from her.

'Look, Luft, we're not partners. We're just temporarily forced to work together. There's a difference.'

'Whatever.' Andie yawned and dropped into Luis's chair. She crossed one long leg over the other, still working on disturbing him. Her granddad had always said the way a woman crossed her legs was the most sensual gesture he could think of — elegant and sexy at the same time. Maybe he was right, she thought, swinging her leg slowly. She felt Benton's eyes on her. She could almost feel heat gathering where his gaze touched. Oh, enough of this nonsense, she thought, rattled.

'Yes, they go all the way up,' she said dryly, suddenly not wanting to flirt when she didn't mean it. The best policy might be to just state her position clearly. Then maybe they could behave like ordinary partners instead of like a man and woman circling each other in the age-old dance of seduction.

His gaze moved to her mocking eyes. 'What did you say?'

'My legs. You were wondering just how long they were, weren't you?'

'Don't be ridiculous. I was thinking you're wasting your time making such a big production out of crossing your legs. I'm not interested.'

'Good, because I'm not interested either,' Andie said.

Luis laughed aloud.

'What's so funny?' Bruce asked, taking a deep breath as he glanced again at her incredible legs. Her tanned legs were bare of hosiery. Her feet, with toenails painted crimson, were clad in leather sandals with three-inch heels.

'Nothing's funny,' Luis said, grinning widely. 'Private joke.'

'Private joke my Aunt Fanny,' he muttered. Luis knew him too well. How he'd ended up having such a ridiculous conversation with Andie — and in front of everyone in the room — was a mystery to him. The woman was impossible. Just when he thought he had control over the situation, she said something so unexpected, it knocked him off balance.

'Glad we agree, Benton,' she said. 'It's a good thing we don't have to worry about sexual attraction interfering with our working relationship.'

'Right. We're definitely on the same wavelength,' he declared. 'We shouldn't have a problem getting this case closed. Then we can both get on with our lives.'

'Good. Aiello miscalculated if he thought we couldn't be professional enough to work together,' she said. 'Score one for us good guys.'

Bruce shut up, trying to figure out

how she'd manipulated him into agreeing that he had no sexual interest in her.

When his phone rang, he grabbed it up. A moment later he covered the mouthpiece and said to Andie, 'Make yourself comfortable, Luft. It's my sister. I'll be a few minutes.'

He'd have hugged Darcy if she'd been standing next to him. Thankful for the respite, he hoped his sister's tale of parental woe would bring him back to reality. That's what he needed before he started fantasizing about Andie again.

'I swear, Bruce,' Darcy said, 'if I'd known a child was so exhausting, I'd have had one sooner. I just don't have the energy I used to.'

'I don't believe you.'

'Tell you what, brother dear. When Chase comes home, baby-sit Sophie so we can have a few hours alone. Then you'll know what I'm talking about.'

Bruce laughed. 'Come on. You're exaggerating. Sophie's just a tiny little girl. She wouldn't even be a challenge for me,' he joked.

'Here I am losing my sanity and you're making light of it. All right. I'm going to insist you baby-sit her. You'll beg for mercy just like me.'

'You do sound pretty frazzled.'

'Between Sophie's terrible threes and this fashion show I agreed to chair, I'm going nuts.'

'I thought that phase kids grow through was called the terrible twos?' Bruce couldn't help but grin.

'In Sophie's case, it was terrific twos and now the terrible threes. I really don't know how such a small child can get into so much trouble. I found the little monkey climbing the shelves in the linen closet yesterday as if it were a ladder!'

The idea of his niece falling sent cold chills through Bruce — and it made him have second thoughts about baby-sitting. 'Maybe you'd better put those childproof doorknobs on the linen closet.'

'Already taken care of. Chase swears

61

he's going to enter a monastery until she's grown.'

'Too bad he didn't do it a few years ago,' Bruce muttered. 'Before he corrupted you.'

'I heard that! You leave Chase alone.' Darcy laughed. 'Besides, I know you do like him so quit pretending you don't.'

Bruce made the mistake of looking at Andie. She was swinging her leg back and forth again. His eyes followed the movement as he became aware of her interest in his conversation. He lost track of what he and his sister had been talking about. All he could think about was Andie's comment about her legs. He swallowed and tried not to think about tracing them all the way up.

'Bruce?' Darcy called. 'You still there?'

Bruce plummeted back to earth. 'Yeah. What did I call you about?'

Darcy laughed. 'You must be wearing your shoulder holster too tight. It's cutting off the circulation to your brain. I called you.'

'Sorry, it's been a rough day here.'

'Overrun with bad guys, huh?'

'Something like that.'

'I wanted to remind you that you, Luis, and Peyton volunteered to help with the fashion show.'

'We did? I don't recall doing something that dumb.'

'You don't? You must be getting old, brother dear.'

Bruce sighed. 'What kind of help?'

'Just as escorts for some of the models. Kind of like animated props. Nothing too demanding.'

'You wouldn't be trying to fix the three of us up with blind dates, would you?'

A smothered laugh from Andie reminded him he had an audience. He frowned at her. She imitated him, and he flushed.

'Bruce, this is me you're talking to — not Mom. I only asked you because I really want Luis and Peyton. They're utterly gorgeous. Just didn't want to hurt your feelings, that's all. You've known Peyton so long, some of his fashion sense should have rubbed off on you.' Darcy sighed.

'What's wrong with the way I dress?' he asked. When Andie laughed, he scowled at her and told his sister, 'Never mind.'

Irritated by the two women, he said, 'Are you the same girl who didn't even own a lipstick three years ago? Now you're one of the fashion police, hosting style shows. Since you married Whitaker, anyone would think you were hoping to get on the cover of *Vogue* or something.'

Darcy laughed. 'Fat chance. But even tomboys eventually grow up, Bruce — when they fall in love.'

'Uh-huh. Got to run, Darcy. I have, uh,' — he caught Andie's amused look — 'some work to do.'

'Will you ask Luis and Peyton?'

'Sure. You can count on them. Me, too. You know the sports camp is important to us too. But don't start matchmaking. You're not very good at it.' Still grinning, he hung up.

'What's this sports camp I heard you mention?' Andie asked.

'It's an annual event for underprivileged kids. My brother-in-law's company — Sunbelt Oil — started it a couple of years ago. This year they wanted to bring in more kids, so my sister's trying to raise the funds by hosting a fashion show and a reception. I understand she approached every energy company in town to get them to sponsor tables.'

'My dad's security company would probably buy a table.' Andie took a piece of paper from Bruce's desk and dashed off a quick note. 'Here's his name and phone number. Tell your sister to call him.'

'Thanks. I'll do that,' Bruce said, surprised at her interest.

He pocketed the note, then turned and called over to Peyton and relayed Darcy's request. With a despairing groan, Peyton dropped his head onto his folded arms. 'What are the chances Darcy just wants us to do what she said? Be escorts for the models?'

'Slim to none,' Bruce answered cheerfully. 'Bet you ten bucks she's got some of her single friends lined up.'

'What's so bad about that?' Andie asked.

'Nothing, if you want to go out with some marriage-hungry career woman whose biological clock is ticking like a time bomb. Frankly, I don't. My sister's got the idea everyone should be happily married, just like her. She's made it her mission to get me, Luis, and Peyton hitched.'

'Yeah, but she's your sister, not mine,' Peyton grumbled. 'So I should be off-limits.'

'Sorry, pal. If she's met you and you're single, you're fair game.'

'Darcy doesn't understand that the three of us are already happy. Why complicate things with commitment and,' — Bruce paused and shuddered dramatically — 'the M thing.'

'Some men actually like being married,' Andie said mildly.

'Name five,' he said. Suddenly, he remembered how she'd looked in the bouffant wedding gown when she'd lifted her skirt, revealing the silk stockings and the garter. Those long legs of hers invited a hand — his hand — to slide over the silk until he touched skin — warm, honey-gold skin. He swallowed hard.

'Never mind,' Andie said. 'If you're finished with personal phone calls, and you don't have any objection to earning your salary, why don't we get down to details?'

Bruce busied himself getting a notepad and a pen. It was either that or grab her out of the chair and kiss her until she begged for more. This was insane. He was insane. He clicked the ballpoint and said, 'Why don't you fill me in on this case?' He clicked the pen a few more times.

When she hadn't answered after a few minutes, he said, 'Luft? Are you going to tell me about this case or do I have to get the facts by ESP?'

'Keep your shirt on. This past year there's been a series of robberies in some of the most exclusive boutiques in San Antone. Mostly designer clothes, including some very expensive wedding dresses.'

Andie paused. 'You're smirking. What's so funny about this?'

He shrugged. 'Why steal a wedding dress? A few hundred bucks here or there isn't a very big score.'

'A few hundred bucks? Sergeant, some of these gowns cost ten thousand or more.'

'Dollars?'

'No, Monopoly money.'

'Anybody would be a fool to pay that much for something to get hitched in.'

'I get the impression you think getting hitched is pretty stupid in general.'

'Hey, you said it, I didn't.'

'The clothes have turned up in odd places. Some were sold in flea markets at cut-rate prices. One was spotted in a bridal registry ad. The photographer for the ad was Pippo Lombardo.'

'The guy who owned the studio where I found you.'

'Exactly. I suspect he's got a smuggling racket going on — disposing of the cheaper items in flea markets in south Texas but probably sending most of the dresses to South America and Europe. A really unique dress — one with lace roses in palest pink and peach and with a tulle over satin skirt — '

'Hey, skip the fashion monologue.'

Andie ignored him, and calmly finished, 'It was the one the model wore in the picture he took.'

'Do you think he's the ringleader?'

'I know so. I just haven't figured out whether his sister is in on it as well. I do know he's stolen tens of thousands of dollars in merchandise. That's what we're out to stop.'

Bruce tossed his pen and pad to the desktop. Shaking his head, he said, 'This case isn't worth the manpower assigned to it. Nor the womanpower either. So what's the angle? There's got to be more to this than you've told me.'

Andie sighed. 'Very good. You're right. It seems that someone close to city government has a sister who's a designer. Her creations have been targeted. It's made such an impact on her business that she's finding it difficult to get insurance now.'

'So somebody called in a favor. That figures.'

'It's still a crime,' Andie insisted.

'Sure, sure.' He was supposed to track down stolen dresses? Ridiculous. There had to be a way out of this trap. 'So how do you want to work this?'

'We'll start with Lombardo's sister Ursula — she's the one who modeled the wedding dress for the advertisement. Then we'll retrace the case — talk to everyone again and see if I can find where he's holed up.'

'You mean see if *we* can find him,' he corrected. With a sigh, he said, 'We may as well start now. Let's go interview the sister.'

'No can do,' Andie said. 'It'll take

longer than an hour to get to the other side of town where Ursula Lombardo lives — and there's no telling how long we'll be talking with her.' She looked at her watch. 'I have to be home by four today.'

'Why? You taking medication or something?'

'No. I have an appointment later this evening,' she hedged, not wanting to tell him the real reason.

'An appointment?' He frowned. 'What kind of appointment?'

'My, but you're nosy,' she parried.

'Hey, partners need to know what's going on with each other. Don't you agree? So tell me.'

After a moment, Andie said, 'You're not going to leave this alone, are you?' He grinned in agreement, and she said, 'Okay, if you must know, I have a date.'

'A date?' Bruce frowned. He hadn't considered she might be dating someone. That should make him feel better. It made her completely off-limits. 'That's not a very good excuse. I don't

71

ask to leave early every time I have a date.'

Andie flushed. 'Look, I'd already arranged this and can't change it. I don't make a habit of this.'

'Yeah, I bet. So this must be a major date,' he fished, 'if you need so much primping time.'

'Let's change the subject,' she said firmly.

'No, I think I want to know more about this. I thought you didn't date.'

'I don't date cops. I never said I didn't date at all.'

'So you're going to put your social life above your work.' Benton shook his head. 'I should have expected as much.'

'What do you mean?' she asked, trying not to sound defensive.

'That's the problem with most women. Their personal lives come before their jobs.'

'That's a rotten, sexist thing to say!'

'Hey, if the high heel fits . . . ' He mocked her with a grin.

'Well, it doesn't. I've never put my

personal life before my job.'

'Yeah? That's exactly what you're doing right now.' Bruce couldn't seem to stop himself. He didn't want her going out with some other guy, he realized. He was in trouble now.

'Fine. Just forget it. I'll stay as long as you do today. No taking off early. Satisfied?' Andie snapped.

He grinned. 'Not yet, but the day's not over.'

'Just shut up and get your jacket.' She looked him up and down. 'I assume you have a jacket to cover those scruffy clothes?'

'Hey, you're not my sister, so quit dissing my wardrobe.'

'Calling clothes like that a wardrobe is like calling a cockroach a cute insect.'

'Calm down, Luft,' Bruce said, so pleased that he'd put a damper on her plans for the evening that he didn't even take offense at her comments. Before the day was over, he'd discover who this guy was. Maybe he'd check him out — make sure he was right for

73

Andie. After all, she was his partner now, whether he liked it or not. So he owed it to her to protect her interests.

'Where are we going, Luft?' he called after her.

She didn't bother turning, just snapped, 'To interview Ursula Lombardo, where else?'

Grinning, he followed her out of the station, marveling at how she could walk that fast in those heels. Her swaying hips mesmerized him. He wondered what she planned to wear tonight.

Maybe it would be a good idea to take a peek at this guy tonight. Just to make sure that — well, it wasn't as if Bruce was interested in her himself. He grinned, wondering if she'd mind.

5

Andie practically jogged to the police garage. It was as if she were trying to outrun the desire that rippled through her as she'd watched Benton's long, strong fingers clicking that pen. She shivered despite the heat. Benton had large hands. She always thought men with large hands were capable of dealing with anything life threw at them. Maybe that was something she'd figured out years ago when she'd been little and all the men in her family seemed so big.

She'd been just fine, thinking about his hands, when she'd suddenly wondered how it would feel for him to touch her. A thrill of awareness had shot through her. Although he obviously didn't feel any of the sexual attraction that had her tied in knots.

Andie reached the police garage

before he did. 'Get a move on, Benton.' She turned and said, 'Move it! You're wasting time.'

'You sound like you're in a hurry to clear this rinky-dink case, Luft. Guess we're both anxious to get back to some real police work. Or is it that you don't want to be late for your date, cupcake?'

'I'm not worried about being late,' she said between clenched teeth, trying hard not to let his needling get to her.

'Aiello might not let you come back,' Benton said, grinning. 'I wish I knew what you did to tick him off — not that it takes much with him.'

'That's for me to know and you to wonder about. I could ask the same question. What did you do to get on his wrong side?'

'Play your cards right, cupcake, and I might tell you before you leave here permanently.'

'Benton, we might as well get one thing straight right now. We'll get along a whole lot better if you quit calling me that asinine name.'

'What? Cupcake? You mean it annoys you?'

Andie knew by his grin that it was designed to. Oh, dear. She was certain if he knew it annoyed her, he'd never stop saying it. She tried to cover her faux pas. 'No, not at all. I just thought your girlfriends might not like it if they knew you called me that.'

'Girlfriends?'

'Hey, everyone knows about you and your harem. Maybe I should just call you Sheik — or how about stud?' She ignored his smirk. 'Is it true the brainless little redhead on the weather channel is your latest conquest?'

'She's not brainless,' he said, forced to defend the woman he'd accused of being exactly that.

'Not if you measure IQ by bra size, I suppose,' Andie said, lengthening her stride once he'd caught up with her.

'My love life is none of your business.'

'Oh, my. Touchy, aren't we?'

'Not really.'

'Well, is she or isn't she your latest?'

'She was. Past tense. History.'

Andie made a tsk-tsk sound. 'She wanted more, huh? What'd you do? Palm her off on one of your pals?'

'What is this? Is there an unauthorized biography of me in the works that I don't know about?'

Andie laughed. 'Take it easy, sweet thing. You're awfully sensitive for such a big boy.' She felt more in control with him on the defensive. That was the way she liked it.

'I can tell this is gonna be a helluva long day!'

Satisfied, Andie smiled demurely. 'Relax, Benton, I'll let you off the hook for now.'

'Why don't we concentrate on this case? Let's get going and see what we can find. Your car or mine?'

'Aiello said he arranged for us to have a car just for the duration of the case. It was seized in a drug bust over on the south side last month.'

Andie signed the vehicle out while

one of the guys from the motor pool went to get it. When he drove up in a vintage navy blue T-Bird, she stared in shock. Absently, she held her hand out for the key. The mechanic chuckled and dropped the key in her outstretched hand.

In horror, Andie stared at the orange fake fur lining the rear window well. She felt queasy and said a quick prayer that the seats weren't covered in the obnoxious fabric. Benton laughed so hard, he had to lean against the car's orange vinyl top.

'Yeah, that was nice of Aiello,' he said, wiping tears from his eyes. 'I can tell he holds you in high regard.'

'How do you know he didn't pick this car with you in mind?' she snapped, reaching for the driver's door.

'Wait a minute, cupcake,' Bruce said, grabbing the door. 'I'm driving.'

'Not in this car you're not,' she snarled, thoroughly put out with Aiello, Benton, and men in general.

'I always drive,' he said with an edge to his voice.

'Well, this time you don't. You get to ride.' Andie smiled sweetly but didn't budge.

'I don't want to ride. I want to drive.'

'Well, we don't always get what we want, now do we?'

He made a grab for the key, but Andie jerked it behind her. When he reached behind her, she whipped it around and buried it in her fist.

Benton leaned against her and tried to remove it from her hand, but she refused to let go. He and Andie engaged in a silent tug of war even as his chest pressed against hers. Startled by the intensity of feeling that shot through her body, Andie's grip on the key loosened. He pried her fingers open and grabbed it. She fought for a minute but suddenly let go. Momentum carried Benton backwards. His arms flailed as he fought for balance.

Andie took the opportunity to slide swiftly into the orange and navy plaid driver's seat. She slammed the door and gripped the steering wheel.

'Get out of there,' he said, flinging open the door.

'I don't think so,' Andie said, smiling smugly.

When he leaned in close, she snatched the key from his hand and inserted it in the ignition. Without batting an eye, she turned the engine over. 'Better get in if you don't want to run alongside all the way to Ursula Lombardo's house.'

Bruce looked at her satisfied smile and knew he'd lost the battle. Laughter struggled with aggravation. For some reason, the scene amused him more than it bothered him, but he didn't reveal that to Andie. She looked too proud of her coup for him to deflate her success. He found his admiration for her increasing.

'Come on, Benton, you're wasting time. Besides, you don't know where she lives, and I do.'

He'd let her win this one, he decided,

walking around and getting in the passenger side. Their next contest would go his way, he vowed. Couldn't have her taking the upper hand in everything. He grinned, already looking forward to next time.

* ★ ★ ★

Andie was careful to keep her expression neutral as Benton slammed the passenger door. *Score one for me*, she thought, mentally chalking up a mark for her side. She watched from the corner of her eye as he buckled his seat belt while she drove to the exit.

'Slow down,' he said as soon as she pulled out of the garage and onto the street.

'I'm not exactly breaking the speed limit,' she retorted. Feeling rather smug, she drove quickly through the fast-moving traffic and after a while, maneuvered up onto 35 East.

Finally, Benton spoke. 'You want to tell me where we're headed?'

'Out to Universal City. Ursula Lombardo has a place out there.'

'I thought you said that she was on the south side?'

'Did I?' Andie flashed him a mischievous grin.

'Don't trust your own partner?' Benton asked. 'What's the matter? Afraid I might locate her, find her brother and close this case before you have a chance to make an arrest?'

'Why, Benton, you make it sound as if I don't trust you,' Andie said. 'But I do. I trust you as much as you trust me.'

To her relief, he didn't pursue that subject. Instead, he asked, 'So you think she knows where he's holed up?'

'Obviously or we wouldn't be trekking out there.'

'What makes you think she'll talk to you?'

'Trust me. She'll talk to me.' At least she hoped Ursula would. 'I'm afraid Ursula isn't going to be very happy when she discovers we bungled her brother's arrest.'

'Oh?'

'Yes. You see, Ursula is scared of Pippo. That's the only reason she told me where to catch him.'

The afternoon rush hour hadn't really started yet, and it didn't take as long for them to get to the suburb north-east of downtown as she'd thought it would.

Andie exited the freeway and took the first right, drove a couple of miles and turned left at the entrance of Air Acres, a subdivision originally designed to house military personnel from Randolph Air Force Base.

Most of the look-alike frame houses were fairly well-maintained, with neat front yards that should have been green but were brown stubble instead, and weathered privacy fences enclosing large backyards.

Though none of the ranch-style houses would ever make the cover of *Architectural Digest*, the one Andie finally parked in front of looked worse than the others on the block. Not a blade of grass, not even a weed, had survived the endless days of heat. White paint peeled from the siding and faded green shutters hung askew from the windows. The stockade-style fence surrounding the backyard looked as if a strong gust of wind would knock it down.

'Let me do the talking,' she said, as she cut the engine.

'Do I have a choice?'

'Not really.'

She gave him a cocky smile and opened the door. Maybe she should give Benton a break, she thought. He'd been quiet on the drive out here. She guessed she'd tormented him long enough.

He pulled the denim sport jacket from the backseat and shrugged into it. Then he followed her up the cracked sidewalk.

By the time they reached the front door, perspiration was trickling down her neck. She turned to say something to Benton and noticed him looking her over — making a big deal of looking her over, in fact. She craned to look at her backside. 'What is it? Did I sit on something in that awful car?'

'No, I was just wondering where your weapon was concealed, Sergeant Luft.'

Andie flushed. 'I can guarantee you it isn't under my skirt, so take your eyes off my hips.'

'Relax, cupcake.'

When she saw his satisfied grin, she got a tight grip on her temper. He was just plotting ways to irritate her. Coolly, she said, 'If it's any of your business, it's in my purse.'

Rattled, but trying not to show it, Andie rang the bell.

'What a disappointment, cupcake. Really interesting holsters made for women these days. I was having so much fun guessing what kind you might be wearing.'

Completely aggravated now, Andie pounded on the door, since she couldn't pound on his thick, chauvinist skull.

Furious barking reached her ears. Startled, she stood on tiptoe and peeked through the tiny window in the door, but she couldn't see anything.

Suddenly something hard slammed against the door. Andie jumped backwards and collided with Benton. She swallowed over the knot of fear in her throat. The barking sounded as if the animal inside planned to come right through the door to grab her.

'What's the matter?' Benton asked, clasping her shoulders.

His touch felt surprisingly good and comforting, Andie thought.

'Afraid of dogs?'

'No. I like dogs — cute, little dogs.' She shuddered. 'Big dogs? Well, they're unpredictable. And territorial.'

Benton patted her shoulders. 'How old were you when you were bit?'

Surprised, Andie looked over her shoulder at him. 'Six,' she said flatly. 'How'd you know?'

'It doesn't take a genius to see you're really scared. That kind of fear usually comes from childhood.'

'Very perceptive, Benton,' Andie said, surprised by his sensitivity. He hadn't wanted to make her feel foolish. She took a deep breath and reluctantly stepped forward. His hands fell away.

'Ursula didn't have a dog the last time I was here.' With her heart pounding nearly in unison with the dog's barks, she knocked on the door again. Abruptly, it opened. Startled, Andie blinked at the brunette who stood there. Ursula Lombardo wore the tiniest bikini Andie had ever seen this side of a Mexican resort. Her right hand gripped the dog's metal-studded leather collar.

Involuntarily, Andie took a hasty step backward. The dog in question was a monster pit bull — the biggest she'd ever seen. She edged back farther until she once again felt Benton's chest against her back. The vicious animal barked unceasingly.

'Shut up, Ralph,' Ursula yelled. 'Quiet!'

Amazingly, the dog fell silent.

Andie found the ragged edges of her attitude and pulled it together. 'Hey, Ursula!' She stepped toward the brunette. A volley of loud barks erupted from the dog.

'Oh, no. Not you again.' The woman sounded more resigned than angry. She shook the dog's collar and shouted, 'I said shut up, Ralph.'

The barks subsided into growls as the dog stared balefully at Andie.

Just then Ursula Lombardo's face broke into a welcoming smile. 'Well, I see you brought company this time. Who's this tall drink of water?'

'This is Sergeant Benton,' Andie said crisply. 'We'd like to ask you a few questions.'

'Well, Sergeant Benton, as long as one of those questions is a request for my phone number, fire away.'

Andie rolled her eyes. 'May we come in out of the heat?'

'Sure, come on.' Ursula held the door wide.

Andie started to step in, but the dog sprang up, ears flat against his head, and dared her to put a foot inside his territory.

'Oh, don't mind Ralph Lauren,' Ursula said. 'He's really well behaved.'

'You named your dog Ralph Lauren?' Benton asked.

'Oh, he's not mine. He belongs to Pippo.' The woman turned to the dog and sternly commanded, 'Sit, Ralph.'

The dog promptly planted its bottom on the floor, but continued to growl, apparently to remind the two visitors that it didn't like them.

'So your brother dropped by yesterday?' Andie asked, excited.

'No. I came home last night and found Ralph in the backyard and a note from Pippo stuck in the back screen door. I thought you were supposed to arrest him,' Ursula complained.

'May we see the note?' Andie asked, ignoring her complaint.

Ursula sighed, sounding as if all the troubles of the world weighed her down. 'Sure. Come on in.' She held the door wide.

Andie took one step and the pit bull went ballistic. She froze. 'Uh, maybe you should put Ralph in the other room. Please?'

The woman didn't answer her. Andie noticed that Ursula was checking out Benton's assets as if she had x-ray vision. In any event, it wasn't difficult to read what was on Ursula's mind as she undressed Benton with her eyes.

'Ursula? The dog?' Andie pleaded.

'I bet your big, strong partner's not scared of little old Ralph,' Ursula gushed as she propped one tanned shoulder against the door frame and stretched her arms overhead in a sensual parody of a yawn. The movement lifted her voluptuous breasts, which threatened to overflow the tiny bikini top. The skimpy bikini bottom slipped a little farther down her hips, revealing a band of white skin way below her navel.

Despite herself, Andie glanced over

to see how Benton was reacting to this display. To her disgust, he was giving the woman a bone-melting smile. He'd never smiled at her like that, she thought, immediately resentful.

'I apologize for dropping in so unexpectedly,' he told Ursula.

'Oh, no problem, Sergeant,' Ursula said, preening in the doorway. 'I was just sunbathing outside on the deck. I needed to come in and reapply my suntan oil anyway. You know it's so hard to get that oil everywhere,' she said suggestively, sounding as breathy as a Marilyn Monroe impersonator. 'Why, I just have the hardest time getting it on my back. I don't suppose you could help me out with that little job, could you, Sergeant?'

'No, ma'am, he couldn't,' Andie snapped. Her anger grew when she saw Benton smile apologetically at Ursula.

'Sorry, Ms. Lombardo. It would definitely be a conflict of interest,' he said in a voice that hinted he'd love to if only his stodgy female partner weren't there.

'We'd surely appreciate it if we could ask you a few questions,' Benton drawled.

'Well, sure,' Ursula said. 'It is so hot today. I swear, it's been so hot lately I just wear nothing most of the time . . . ' She hesitated a split second, then added, 'Except for my swimsuit bottom, of course.'

Good grief! Could the woman be any more obvious, Andie thought. 'Thanks, Ursula. We appreciate it.' She started to step past the woman again, but the dog sprang to its feet and barked. Andie halted, disliking the dog nearly as much as she suddenly detested Ursula Lombardo. 'Quiet, Ralph!' she yelled.

To her surprise, the dog shut up. Andie supposed attitude worked on dogs, too. She walked past the dog as if he didn't scare the bejeebers out of her.

'Don't mind him, Ms. Luft. He's like most men, putty in your hands once you know how to handle him.' Ursula pranced into the living room.

'And I bet you know that from experience,' Andie muttered as she followed.

'Well, I've had my share,' Ursula said archly. 'As long as I'm here, Ralph won't bother you. He's just a teddy bear.' She bent down and took Ralph's head in her hands and shook it side to side. 'Aren't you, baby? Just a big ol' teddy bear.'

Ursula waited until Benton walked past her. She pretended to trip and fall against him. Both his hands came up and grabbed her upper arms to steady her. Andie watched Ursula Lombardo 'accidentally' brush her breasts against Benton's chest.

'Oh, excuse me, Sergeant.' Ursula giggled and gave him a sexy smirk she must have spent her high school years practicing.

'No problem, ma'am,' Bruce said.

When he glanced over at Andie and winked, she crossed her eyes and made a face at him. *Real mature, Andie,* she scolded herself, as she sat on the blue vinyl couch.

6

Bruce sat on the love seat opposite the couch and wasn't surprised when Ursula plopped her bikini-clad body right next to him. The woman squirmed and wiggled until she was just inches away from him. Smiling, she leaned toward him, treating him to another glimpse of her rather spectacular cleavage.

Before Andie could ask the first question, Ursula giggled and asked, 'Are you her boyfriend or something, Sergeant?'

He smiled. 'No, ma'am.'

'He's my partner,' Andie grated. 'Now, may we see the — '

'Partner?' Ursula echoed, batting her eyes at Benton. 'So are you her single partner, Sergeant Benton?'

'Yes, ma'am.'

'Well, isn't that nice,' Ursula said, her voice huskier, more intimate. She looked him over once more. By the time her eyes met his, Bruce figured she could probably guess his briefs size. The woman was obviously an expert at the art of mentally undressing a guy.

To his amusement, Andie stared daggers at him and Ursula. When she noticed him looking, she made a great show of studying the room. It was a sight to behold, what with green shag carpet from thirty years ago. The vinyl couch, love seat, and club chair must once have been bright blue. Now the arms and seats were a dingy grayish color with cracked piping and missing buttons. The whole room was frozen in time — complete with a framed *Saturday Night Fever* movie poster.

Bruce wondered if the guy who'd named his dog after a famous designer nearly barfed every time he visited here. He actually felt a shred of sympathy for the photographer. Maybe Pippo could plead temporary insanity — driven to a crime spree by environmental pressures.

Grinning, he decided to get the interview going so they could get out of there before Ursula Lombardo tore his clothes off and had her way with him.

'The note, Ursula?' he asked.

'Oh, yeah. The note.' She stood, turned to Ralph and said sternly, 'Stay.' She made a vertical movement with her hand in front of the dog's nose and repeated the command. Then she swayed out of the room.

Ralph immediately stood. The hackles on his neck rose as he growled at Andie and took a step toward her.

'Benton!' she gasped.

'Take it easy. Just be still. Don't show fear.'

'Easy for you to say,' Andie hissed.

Ursula pranced back into the room. She handed a yellow piece of paper to Benton. Aloud, he read, 'Got to leave town. Take care of Ralph. I'll settle with you later.'

'That's it?' Andie asked, sounding disappointed.

'Not even a signature,' Bruce said,

handing the note back to Ursula. She folded it into a tiny square and tucked it into the left cup of her bra top.

'Do you have any idea where he is?' Andie asked.

'Not a clue,' Ursula said, sounding cheerful. 'If I'm lucky, he won't be back. Ralph is much better company than Pippo. He doesn't steal from me, and he doesn't go around complaining about my decor.' She patted the dog and let it slobber all over her hand. 'Why didn't you arrest my brother?'

Bruce intercepted a nasty look from Andie. She looked as if she could have chewed nails and spit them at the woman. 'There was a little snafu, and your brother got away.'

'I told you he was slippery,' she said triumphantly to Andie.

'I don't suppose you'd know anyone he may have gone to?' Andie asked with barely concealed hostility.

'No, Sergeant Luft, like I told you last time. Pippo and I don't exactly get along. I don't know his artsy-fartsy friends, and I don't want to. He'll turn up when he needs something. He always does.'

Andie asked her a few more questions about Lombardo's hangouts and his pals, but Ursula pleaded ignorance on each one.

They stood. Bruce handed her his card. She touched his sleeve and cooed, 'Oh, Sergeant! Is this your personal phone number?'

'It's my pager. You can reach me anytime.'

'Day or night?' she asked, batting her eyes and leaning forward so he'd have a farewell view of her cleavage.

Benton smiled. 'Yes. Day or night. If you hear from your brother, I'd appreciate it if you gave me a call.'

'Sure thing,' she said, tapping the card against her lips. Then holding his gaze, she ran the tip of her tongue around her crimson mouth and tucked the card into her bikini top.

From the corner of his eye, he saw Andie open her purse. He wondered if she planned to pull out her weapon and plug Ursula or him out of frustration. Instead, she pulled out a card and handed it to Ursula without saying a word. Ursula looked at it, then opened her fingers and let it drift to the floor.

'Thanks for your time, ma'am,' Bruce said.

'Anytime, Sergeant. And I do mean that. Anytime — day or night.'

* * *

At the car, Bruce didn't quibble over who was going to drive. He figured Andie needed something to occupy her hands to keep her from launching a full attack on him. Once in the car, she fired it up and drove to the end of the cul-de-sac to turn around. Then with a squeal of the tires, she roared away.

'Take it easy. This old buggy isn't used to being driven like a race car,' Bruce said, amused but knowing he shouldn't let her see it.

'Maybe I'm in a hurry,' she said.

'Oh, yeah, I forgot about that hot date of yours.'

She withered him with a look.

'Good thing I was along,' she muttered after a bit.

'What do you mean?'

'If I hadn't been there, she'd have had you tied down to the couch. Probably would have used that mean dog to make sure you gave her what she wanted.'

'You think so?' Bruce felt a quiet satisfaction fill him. Andie Luft wasn't immune to him. To sound this jealous, she had to be interested.

'No doubt about it. Guess she goes for sloppy-dressed cops.'

'That's kind of a left-handed compliment.'

Andie snorted. 'You were disgusting — flirting with her like that. It was completely unprofessional.'

'I didn't flirt with her.'

'What do you call it?'

'Taking advantage of a witness's natural interest to win her cooperation?'

'Whatever you call it, it was unprofessional.'

'Like you haven't used your feminine wiles to get a suspect to play ball?'

'Never!'

'Well, everybody does it. Smile, play nice, lead him on a little.'

'Play nice? Is that what you call it? Well, let me tell you something, partner. You've got playing nice down to a fine art.'

'You're just mad because she talked to me instead of to you.'

Andie swerved around a slow-moving car. 'I am not mad.'

'Maybe you're jealous then.'

'Jealous? Of what? That man-hungry bimbo back there? Oh, that's rich,' Andie scoffed, knowing that he was absolutely right. She hadn't liked the way the woman looked at him. Rubbed up against him. Talked to him. In short, she hadn't liked Ursula Lombardo laying a finger on her partner.

'You'll have to forgive me if I'm protective of my partner,' she said. 'It goes with the territory. So get used to it.'

'Would you please slow down!' He gripped the dashboard with both hands as she barreled up the entrance ramp to the freeway.

'If you don't like the way I'm driving, tough.'

'I'm going to do the driving next time,' he said. 'If I live that long.'

'Don't bet on it,' she tossed at him. 'I don't know why you're complaining. I'm a good driver.' Andie noticed the speedometer needle hit eighty-five and eased back on the accelerator a little. Maybe she was a tad overwrought.

'I just need to get home quickly,' she said by way of explanation.

'Oh, yeah. The Date.'

Andie told herself not to rise to the bait.

After a few minutes, Bruce asked, 'So where are you going tonight?'

'What?'

'Tonight. The Date. Where are you going?'

She pretended she hadn't heard him.

When he repeated the question, she snapped, 'To Bertolucci's, if it's any of your business.'

'Bertolucci's, huh? That's about fifty bucks a head so the guy at least has good taste and some money. Or a pocket full of plastic. Which is it? Green bucks or plastic?'

'If you must know, he's quite comfortable.'

'Quite comfortable? Ahhh.'

'And what does that mean?'

'Nothing.'

'You think I'm dating him just because he has money?'

'Did I say that?'

'You didn't have to.' She jerked the wheel to the right and floored it, getting around a slow-moving dump truck.

After a few more miles passed, Benton asked, 'Who is he?'

Andie didn't want to answer. 'That's none of your business.'

'Hey, we're partners, remember? Don't partners tell each other everything?'

'You may be my partner, but you're not my teen diary.'

'Aw, come on, Luft. What's the matter? Ashamed of him?'

'Certainly not!'

'Is he some dweeb your best friend fixed you up with?' Bruce grinned. 'Or worse; maybe he's some old geezer your dad dug up.'

'Don't be ridiculous. I can get dates without anyone fixing me up. Unlike someone I could name who depends on his sister to help with his love life.'

'Hey, Darcy doesn't do that. In case you're worried, I do just fine without her.'

'Yeah. I've heard.'

'Now, you and your dweeb. I can just imagine what he looks like,' Bruce continued, ignoring her protests. 'Since you don't date cops because you don't want to get serious about someone in a risky profession — even if it's your own profession which makes no sense at all — I imagine you look for some boring guy who's never taken a risk in his life.

The stiffest thing about him is probably the starch in his white shirts.'

'You're being crude and offensive.'

'Hey, I was referring to his backbone. You've just got a dirty mind.'

Andie's knuckles showed white where she gripped the steering wheel.

'I bet he drives a minivan too. No dangerous wheels for him!'

Stung, Andie retorted, 'Wade drives a perfectly acceptable Lexus.'

'A Lexus, huh?' Benton laughed long and hard. 'What is he? A scumbag lawyer?'

Incensed, Andie nearly shouted, 'He's a very nice CPA.'

'A very nice CPA?' Bruce echoed. Then he erupted in laughter.

Andie wished she'd kept her mouth shut. Benton seemed to bring out the worst in her personality.

He wiped his eyes when his laughter finally faded. 'Are you going to discuss mutual funds over drinks?'

She whipped off the freeway, braking on the exit ramp, then roared down onto the surface street. If she managed to get to HQ before she pulled over and did bodily harm to Benton, she thought, it would be a miracle.

'Later, you can ask him in for a nightcap,' Benton continued. 'Maybe you could check out a sexy video.' He snapped his fingers. 'I know just the one! How about *Debbie Does Dallas — and The 1040 Form*.' He laughed at his own joke.

Andie was hard-pressed not to laugh too. That was pretty funny, but she managed to hide her amusement.

A few minutes later, she whipped into the garage and took the first empty space. She brought the car to a screeching halt. Relief poured through her. She'd be on her way in minutes and wouldn't have to put up with Benton's beguiling laughter and his disturbing presence any longer.

'See you tomorrow,' she said as she climbed out of the navy T-Bird. It pinged and rattled before the engine finally died.

'What's your hurry, Luft? I think we should go to the office and write up a report.'

Her mouth dropped. 'Are you seriously nuts?'

'No. Proper procedure. We need to type up our notes while they're fresh in our mind.'

'Hey, I'm on to your game, Sergeant. You're just trying to make me late for my date!'

'Now, why would I want to do that?'

She shook her head. 'Darned if I know, but you do.'

'I'm just being professional. Weren't you the one complaining because you thought I was unprofessional? Now who's being unprofessional?'

Andie refused to answer.

'I just want to show you that I'm a pro — the ultimate pro.'

'Fine. Go type up your notes. Type as many as you want to. I'm leaving.'

'Tsk, tsk, tsk,' Bruce said.

'Don't do that. I hate it when people do that.'

'I'm really disappointed in you,' he said.

She rolled her eyes.

'I mean, you really convinced me your job was important to you. More important than an overpriced dinner with some loser like your dweeb boyfriend.'

'Benton, do you work at being a jerk or does it just come naturally?'

He smiled the same kind of smile he'd given Ursula Lombardo. Andie felt its warmth penetrate her and heat up her libido — which she didn't want heated — at least not by him. He wasn't The One. He couldn't ever be The One. He was a cop!

He winked at her. 'It's a gift, pard, a pure and simple gift.'

He took her arm and half dragged her to the office.

With a sigh, Andie followed, noting that nearly everyone had gone for the day. A glance at her wristwatch told her she could spend no more than ten minutes here if she wanted to be dressed by the time Wade arrived. No nap, no shampoo, no manicure — just a quick shower and a change of clothes.

'All right, all right,' she grumbled.

'Here, you sit in my chair,' Benton said, pulling it out for her.

Suspiciously, Andie eyed the chair. 'You want me to sit in your chair?'

'Why, sure, pard.'

Warily, she sank onto the chair while Benton pulled Luis's over and dropped onto it.

'Paper's in the drawer next to the typewriter.'

'What?' Andie squawked.

'Paper. You need it for the report.'

She stared at him in amazement. 'You sneak! You want me to type it up?'

'Hey, I figured you could do it faster than I could.'

'And why would you think that?'

'Well, you are a woman, after all.'

'What's that got to do with it?'

'All women know how to type.'

Andie didn't hesitate nor bat an eye.

'Not me,' she lied, opening her eyes wide with innocence.

He stopped grinning. 'You're kidding!'

'Not at all. I never learned.'

He eyed her suspiciously. 'So who's going to type up these reports?'

'Guess that leaves you. Pard.' Feeling better at turning the tables on him, she rose, even managed a grin for him. 'If you'll excuse me, I've got a date waiting.'

She waltzed away but stopped at the door, turned and gave him a little wave. 'Don't work too late, Mr. Ultimate Pro.'

'Yeah, give my regards to the dweeb CPA,' he grumbled.

'Very funny.' Andie sighed dramatically. 'I should have known it was a mistake to reveal anything personal to you.'

'Oh, come on, Luft. Lighten up. Trust me.'

She studied him for a long moment. 'No.'

7

Bruce gripped the wrought-iron railing on his balcony. If someone had told him it was possible to fall head over heels for a woman in two weeks, he'd have said they were nuts. Certifiable! But it had happened — and to him of all people.

He turned and paced the length of his balcony, turned and retraced his steps. Two weeks had passed and somehow he and Andie had adapted to each other. He enjoyed her company. She was funny and smart and a damn good cop. He rubbed the nape of his neck. He'd found himself looking forward to seeing her each day and delaying the time they parted. If she'd been anyone else, he'd have already had her in his bed. But for the first time in his life, he was scared to ask a woman out. He was afraid Andie would say no.

Then their friendship would suffer.

With an exasperated mutter, he stared at the cordless phone in his right hand. He shouldn't do this. He knew he shouldn't. But Andie was going out again with that Wade. It was making him crazy. To Bertolucci's — again.

'This is a stupid idea,' he muttered. His voice sounded loud in the quiet of early evening. Normally, swimmers splashed in the pool three stories below his balcony, but it was too hot even for that activity tonight.

He stopped his restless pacing and punched in a number on the phone. As he hit the last number, he cursed and pressed the disconnect button, then began pacing again. His attraction to Andie was eroding his self-control. Everything she did, from the way she walked to the way she gnawed her bottom lip when she was anxious, made him want to pull her into his arms and kiss her until she admitted they were made for each other.

After three steps, he stopped and

braced his hands on the railing again. His shoulders sagged. 'Aw, hell! I give up,' he muttered. He'd just do it. It was no big deal. He was just curious to see what kind of guy Andie Luft considered an acceptable date. Yeah, that was it. Curiosity plain and simple.

He punched in the number again. When his sister answered, he said, 'Hey, Darcy, I was thinking about how frazzled you've sounded lately. Since Chase is out of town again, I thought you might appreciate dinner with an adult.'

'Oh, I don't know. I'm almost too tired to dress to go out.'

'Aw, come on. Keep me company. I'll let you drive the Olds 442 sometime.'

'You'd really let me drive it? When?'

'Well, sometime,' he hedged, not really wanting anyone to drive his toy.

His sister laughed. 'Oh, no. I want a specific day so I'll know you won't try to weasel out of it.'

'Okay. The Sunday after your fashion show.'

'That's a bribe I can't refuse. You win.'

'Can you get a sitter for Sophie?'

'Sure. Chase's parents are in town. I know they'd be thrilled to spoil Sophie for a couple of hours.'

'Great. We haven't had any . . . any quality time or a chance to talk since forever.'

'Quality time? Are you feeling all right?'

Bruce realized he might be laying it on too thick. 'I just thought a nice dinner at Bertolucci's would perk you up. And you know how I love their portobello chicken. So if you're game, why don't we make an evening of it?'

Darcy laughed. 'Ah, food! Now that sounds more like the brother I know and love. But why take me? What happened to your weather girl?'

'We broke up a while back. You were right. She was too young for me.' Bruce hadn't even thought about his former girlfriend or any other woman since he'd met Andie.

'She's too young for anyone with a brain.'

They agreed to meet at the restaurant. Bruce called Bertolucci's next. Since the dinner crowd was usually light during the week, he had no problem getting reservations.

He grinned, imagining Andie's expression when he and Darcy walked in. What would Andie be wearing? he wondered. Something short, he hoped. Maybe one of those little black dresses and very sheer hosiery with high heels. He'd like to see her legs shown off that way. And if the guy she was dating seemed a good match for her, then he wouldn't interfere. But if the dweeb wasn't suitable . . . then Andie was fair game.

Despite everyone's disparaging comments about his clothes, Bruce did have a decent wardrobe. He pulled out the Italian-tailored charcoal suit — after all, Darcy had told him it made his eyes look fantastic — and paired it with his most expensive silk tie.

Whistling, he headed to the shower

with thoughts of his partner dancing in his head.

★ ★ ★

Andie switched off the blow-dryer and spent a few minutes using the curling iron to tame her blond curls. The heat of the day seemed to linger despite the cooling shower and an hour's distance from her partner. She couldn't seem to cool down, though, physically or emotionally. Spritzing cologne over her body helped a little.

Bluntly, she faced the fact that Benton made her hot and bothered — and not just with anger. Every day her desire for him seemed to double, making her feel weak in the knees when he said good morning each day.

Her partner had turned into a major problem. If only she could locate Lombardo, she'd be able to make the arrest and close the case. That was her only salvation from spending day after day with Benton, but it wasn't likely to happen. Pippo seemed to have vanished from the face of the earth. But he was a minor concern compared to her feelings for Benton.

What was she going to do about him? If only he were a bad cop, it would be easy to blow him off. Trouble was, he was an excellent cop and would make anyone a good partner. Her respect for him had grown right along with her feelings for him. She'd never met a man before who appealed to her so much.

Now, to make matters worse, she thought as she applied her makeup, Benton had been absolutely on target about her current boyfriend. Wade was a sweetheart, so kind and nice. Andie sighed with real regret as she pulled on sheer black pantyhose. Nice and so danged boring, but she'd continued dating him because of Benton's gibes. Somehow Wade was a barrier against Benton.

The inevitable couldn't be postponed any longer. She was determined to end her relationship with Wade tonight. It wasn't fair to string him along, Andie told herself as she stepped into her three-inch black heels, then slipped the lined black silk dress over her head. She wore no jewelry other than a pair of diamond studs that matched the flash of light from the tiny rhinestones dotting the ankle straps of the shoes.

Satisfied with her reflection, she trudged downstairs to wait. Since Wade always arrived promptly, she had ten minutes to spare.

From the stairs, she saw her grandfather playing solitaire in the living room. Andie stopped. She felt like creeping back up the stairs until the doorbell rang. Nolan Luft looked up just then.

'Well, is that a frown on little Andie's face?' he called out.

Andie forced a smile. 'Not at all, Granddad.' She didn't want to listen again to his opinion of Wade, or any of the other men she dated.

He slanted his head to the right and studied her. 'You look gorgeous, doll-face. But you are definitely frowning behind that smile.'

Andie sighed. 'I'm just tired. I had a long day at work.'

'Still no luck locating that photographer?' he asked, slapping a card on top of an ace.

'Nope,' she said, disgusted. 'I think he must have been beamed up by aliens.'

Nolan chuckled. 'Hang in there. You'll get him eventually.' He gathered the cards and shuffled them. 'I noticed you got in a half hour later than normal.'

Andie wondered if he kept a diary of everyone's activities. Her grandfather always seemed to know to the minute when she left home each morning and when she returned in the evening. She never had been able to put anything over on him — or the other men in her household. It was like having six guardians watching over her. Sometimes it made her feel loved and protected, and sometimes, like one of those people on the new wave of reality shows whose every move was recorded by videocams. Not that the male Lufts tried to interfere with her life. Much.

'You going out with that Wade again, aren't you?'

'Don't start, Granddad,' she scolded. 'Wade is a very nice young man.'

'Nice! Ha. You're twenty-six years old. What do you want nice for?'

'Granddad!' Andie shook her head. Sometimes she thought she was the only sane member of this family.

'If your grandmother had wanted nice, you wouldn't be sitting here, dollface, because she'd never have married a swabbie like me.' For a moment, his tone lost its jocularity.

Andie leaned down and kissed his cheek. 'Marrying you was the best thing Grandmom ever did — for you and for her. And that's what she always used to say.'

'Sometimes I walk outside and expect to see her working in one of her flowerbeds.' Nolan looked away a moment, coughed, and cleared his throat. 'It doesn't seem possible that she's gone.'

'I know.' The pain in her grandfather's voice matched the pain she felt in her heart. Her grandmother Laura had been the closest thing to a mother Andie could remember after her mom had died in a car crash when Andie was ten. 'I miss her too.'

She saw tears glaze her grandfather's eyes. She couldn't stand to see him reduced to such sadness. Her grandfather had been like a mighty oak in her life.

'Let me tell you about my day,' she said. Soon she had Nolan laughing with a description of her and Benton checking out one of the wedding chapels on their list, looking for any connection to Lombardo.

Nolan gathered up all the cards and shuffled. The cards flew as he used various fancy methods of shuffling, blending, and stacking. Andie had been five years old when he'd taught her how to handle the cards like a Las Vegas dealer. She'd been ten when she'd finally beaten him at draw poker. He hadn't lost his touch, she noticed.

'This Benton sounds more like your kind of guy, dollface. Why don't you invite him over for dinner?'

'Oh, no! Never. He's nothing like what I want in a man. He's opinion-ated, arrogant, and full of himself. Besides, he's a cop.'

'Yeah, I can see why you wouldn't want to date him,' he said dryly, dealing the cards out for another game of solitaire. 'He sounds too much like you.'

'He's a playboy who doesn't know how to be — ' Andie broke off when her grandfather's comment finally sank in. 'Just exactly what is that supposed to mean?'

Nolan Luft shrugged. 'Honey, every cop I've ever known has that kind of self-assuredness. Doesn't matter whether they're military police like me, a cop like your dad, or members of the alpha-bet soup like your brothers. You're like

that, too. We call it attitude. Put a nega-
tive spin on it, and you get called arrogant
and opinionated. But if you look at it in
a positive light . . . ' He shrugged. 'A
good cop has to be sure of himself,
confident. Maybe arrogance is in the
eye of the be-holder.'

Andie gnawed her lower lip. She
knew he was right, but she was certain
that Benton had no interest in her.
Especially since she'd told him where
she stood. Finally, she said, 'Well,
maybe you're right, but I don't have
any interest in dating a cop. You know
what kind of life my mother had
— always worrying about Daddy.'
Benton had made her think about that
a lot and question her judgment.
Maybe it was time to change her policy.

Nolan didn't say anything, just
flipped an ace over and started a row
with it. 'Well, one of these days you're
going to wake up and decide you want
a real man. These blow-dried, hair-
sprayed accountants and lawyers you've
been dating for the last few years don't

qualify. And that's that.'

The doorbell rang, ending their argument. When Andie let Wade in, she noticed that his hair was perfect — unusual in a city where the wind blew nearly all the time, regardless of the season.

Absently she lifted her cheek for his hello kiss. The touch of his lips did nothing to excite her. She'd never really thought before about his hair spray usage. Now she did, comparing his perfect coiffure to Benton's untidy straight black hair. She'd watched Benton rake his fingers through his hair more than once — and wanted to do it herself. No matter how she compared Benton and Wade, Benton always came out on top. Dismayed, she said quickly, 'Let me get a wrap.'

'Sure. I'll chat with your grandfather,' Wade said, smiling his nice smile at her.

That wasn't such a good idea. Her granddad usually did his best to shock Wade. As she dashed up the stairs,

Andie heard Wade ask, 'How are you, Mr. Luft, sir?'

She grabbed the black silk velvet shawl from the armoire and hurried back down.

Nolan had risen to greet Wade. He was saying, 'I'm fine, thanks. You?'

Andie relaxed.

'I'm just fine. Actually, I'm sitting on top of the world right now.' Wade turned and smiled as she hurried into the room. 'Andrea and I are celebrating my most recent achievement. I bagged a mid-seven figure account last week.'

'Really? Did Andrea' — the way her grandfather mimicked Wade's tone made her wince — 'tell you she nearly made a felony arrest a few weeks ago?'

'Wade, shouldn't we be going? When is that reservation for?' Andie interrupted, giving her grandfather a stern look. Unfortunately, the rascal totally ignored it.

Nolan smiled and rocked back on his heels. 'Yep, she beat the crap out of somebody who interrupted her arrest

— probably cracked a rib or two. She ever tell you how she took down two bikers in a dive on the south end of town?'

'Uh, no.' Wade frowned. 'No, she hasn't. Andrea doesn't talk much about her work.' He turned to Andie. 'Did you really beat someone up?' He sounded appalled.

'She sure did. One guy pulled a piece, and she nearly made him eat it for dinner.'

'Don't wait up, Granddad,' Andie called, gripping Wade's arm and practically dragging him away. Why did her grandfather always try to point out the differences between her police work and the much more sedate careers of the men she dated? As if she were more of a man than her dates?

'Good night, sir,' Wade said.

He still sounded shocked, Andie thought, exasperated at her grandfather's not-so-subtle method of discouraging the men in her life.

They walked outside. In the dusk of

early evening, she thought perhaps she was hallucinating. Instead of Wade's lovely gold Lexus, a gray station Wagon sat in the driveway. Andie closed her eyes, then opened them again, but the dorkmobile remained in the driveway. It was as if Benton had forecast the future. In disbelief, she stared at the utilitarian station wagon parked there. It looked like a box on wheels. Aghast, she turned to Wade. 'Where's your car?'

'This is it!' Wade beamed. 'Isn't she a beauty? So how do you like my new wheels?' Without waiting for an answer, he gushed, 'Don't you love her?'

'But . . . what happened to your Lexus?' Andie asked, feeling faint.

'Oh, it wasn't nearly large enough for all the things I haul around. I've got boxes of brochures and folders for the presentations I make. I got tired of dragging them in and out of a small car trunk so I decided to get something more practical.'

He held his arms wide. 'Well, what do you think?'

Andie didn't know what to say. 'Uh, it — that is, she, she's very . . . uh, very,' she gasped out the only word that came to mind, 'nice.'

'Hey, she's more than nice. Great gas mileage for a vehicle this size and one of the best safety records, according to insurance statistics. Less risk of injury in head-on collisions as well as side-impact accidents. As a police-woman you should appreciate that.'

'Police officer,' she said absently.

'What?'

'Women cops prefer to be called police officers. Policewoman is passé.'

'Oh, of course. I beg your pardon. I'll remember that in the future.'

Silently, Andie allowed Wade to escort her to the passenger side. He opened the door, and she slid onto the gray leather seat.

When Wade had seated himself and carefully buckled his seat belt, he reached into his coat pocket and pulled out an expensive gold pen and a notepad.

'What are you doing?'

'Making note of the proper term of address for women police officers.' He flashed her a grin. 'Details are important.'

Andie rolled her eyes. His habit of note taking hadn't bothered her before, but now she wondered if he ever did anything spontaneous and impetuous. No wonder he got on her grandfather's nerves.

When he finished, Wade checked the rearview mirror before slowly and carefully reversing down the driveway.

Andie sighed. This was definitely her last date with Mr. Nice. As if she needed validation that she'd made the right decision, the dull-as-dishwater station wagon — and that darned notepad — provided it. Knowing she planned to dump him, she tried her best to be agreeable. Smiling, she asked, 'Did you trade the Lexus in for this?'

'Yes.' He smiled. 'First, of course, I read all the consumer reports about the different vehicles and details about the many options. When I finished, I knew this was the one I wanted,' he said proudly. 'I might sacrifice a little in panache, but the excellent safety record more than makes up for it, don't you think?'

'Yes, I guess so,' she murmured. A station wagon. A shudder of distaste swept through her. There was little difference between a station wagon and a minivan. She thought of the powerful, black-on-black 4×4 pickup Benton drove. Thank goodness her partner wasn't around to comment on her date's new vehicle.

'You look very nice tonight, Andrea.'

'Thank you, Wade.' Andie looked at him and began to wonder how she'd endured their previous dates. True, his blond hair was appealing, thick and wavy beneath the hair spray. He was tall and well built and dressed well — although conservatively.

Andie suddenly realized she'd never seen him in anything but a suit and tie.

What would he look like in worn jeans, a faded T-shirt, and scuffed running shoes?

'You seem preoccupied,' Wade said.

'Oh, I'm sorry. Did you ask me something?'

'I was just telling you about my day. What were you thinking about?'

'Oh, um, work,' Andie said, waving her hands as if the subject were of no importance. 'I'm sorry.'

'Tell me more. I realized after your grandfather brought it to my attention that you have never really talked about your job. I always seem to do the talking. I know you're with the police department — hardly a usual job for a beautiful woman.'

His attempt at flattery sounded patronizing and rubbed her the wrong way.

She didn't want to talk about her job with him. 'I'm in Robbery. I started at one of the substations in patrol. When I was assigned to Robbery, I thought I'd be transferred to Main Headquarters, but the department decentralized Robbery and parceled everyone out to the substations so I've remained where I started. Recently I was assigned downtown to work on a special case.' Most civilians didn't understand what it was like to be a cop, and what it meant to be a woman cop was even more misunderstood. Dating outside the department usually allowed her to leave work at the station.

'Do you have a partner?'

Andie laughed. 'That's kind of a sore subject. I'm temporarily shackled to another officer.'

'What's wrong with her?'

'Not her. Him. I'd rather not go into it.' She definitely didn't want to discuss Benton with Wade.

8

A short while later Wade pulled under the canopy at Bertolucci's. A parking valet hurried over and helped Andie out. She smiled and murmured a quick thank-you.

When Wade walked around with measured steps, she took his proffered arm. They strolled into the restaurant. She imagined they made a nice-looking couple. That thought made a giggle bubble inside her. *Nice*.

Quiet strains of violin music floated through the air. That too was nice, she thought, fighting the insidious desire to giggle.

The maitre d' seated them quickly at a table in front of a floor-to-ceiling window facing a courtyard. Andie glanced around the room. There were few other diners at the white, linen-covered tables. She glanced out the window at the tiled courtyard. In the center, water gurgled from a bronze fish in a fountain. Different varieties of fern and ivy surrounded the fountain, creating an atmosphere of serenity.

Andie took a deep breath and let the calm wash away her edginess. 'I adore this place,' she said. 'Thanks for bringing me here again.'

'It is very nice, and you're welcome,' Wade said, taking the wine list the sommelier held out. Wade frowned as he studied it.

Andie struggled with another fit of giggles but managed to control herself. She knew Wade fancied himself a connoisseur. Personally, she didn't much care for wine, but she hadn't told him that. Her attention wandered to the maitre d', who was leading a couple to the table next to theirs.

The woman caught her interest first. She was, in a word, stunning. As tall as her companion and with black hair that cascaded over her shoulders and fell like a shining curtain to her waist, she wore a strapless red sheath that was to die for.

Definitely the kind of woman who walked into a room and turned heads — unlike Andie. At that moment, the woman laughed at something her escort said. She seemed happy, too, which made Andie, by comparison, feel even moodier.

Andie lifted her water glass and sipped. At precisely that moment she recognized the man whispering to the statuesque woman. Sheer jealousy took her breath away, and the water went down the wrong pipe.

Andie coughed and coughed. She couldn't seem to stop. Grabbing her napkin, she covered her mouth, wanting to hide behind it, so no one — especially Bruce Benton — could see what she knew must be a red, splotchy face.

Tears swam in her eyes. Still she could see Benton rise from his chair and step over to her table. Oh, no!

'Why, Andie! Fancy meeting you here,' he said.

She coughed some more and tried to give him a nasty look but with teary eyes and a scarlet face, she was certain it didn't look very menacing.

Benton pounded her on the back. 'Are you all right?' He crouched next to her chair in a most solicitous manner.

Andie glared at him and wanted to tell him where he could take his worried expression. Instead, she nodded, still unable to speak.

'Do you know this man, Andrea?' Wade asked, looking more concerned about the propriety of a strange man accosting them than anything else. She nodded in answer.

Bruce looked over at Wade. 'I'm Sergeant Bruce Benton, San Antonio Police Department. Andrea is my partner. And you are?' he asked in his official voice.

What did Andie see in this guy? he wondered as her date rose and introduced himself. The guy really was a dweeb. Well, maybe he had the looks to attract women, Bruce conceded reluctantly, but he wasn't the kind of guy that Andie needed.

By this time Bruce's companion had risen and come over also. 'Why don't you two back off and give her some air,' she very sensibly suggested. To Andie, she said, 'Why don't we go to the powder room? You need a touch-up.'

Gratefully, Andie nodded and rose, following the woman without question, if for no other reason than curiosity.

* * *

'So you're Wade?' Bruce asked, dropping into Andie's chair.

Wade looked at him cautiously. 'Right. And you're the temporary partner?'

Bruce nodded and gestured to the waiter. 'Women! No telling how long those two will be gone. You don't mind if I get a drink while we're waiting for the ladies, do you?'

'Not at all. In fact, I'll have a glass of sherry.'

'Sherry? You actually drink sherry?'

'It's really quite good. Would you like to try a glass?'

Bruce held up both hands as if warding off some evil. 'No, no. A beer will do fine.'

After the waiter had taken their orders, Bruce asked, 'How long have you known Andie?'

'Andie doesn't really fit her, you know. Andrea is much more proper and ladylike. Just like her.'

'Proper? Ladylike?' Bruce nearly choked. Ladylike was not an adjective he'd have used to describe his new partner. Irritating, yes. Easily irked, definitely. Sexy and desirable also leapt to his mind. But ladylike? This guy didn't know beans about Andie Luft.

'Andrea and I are celebrating our fifth anniversary tonight.'

'Five years?' Bruce felt as if someone had punched him in the gut.

'No, five dates,' Wade said, smiling.

Bruce felt as if a burden had been lifted, but Wade's next comment brought the anxiety back.

'But I could easily visualize five years.'

His dreamy voice disturbed Bruce. 'Not if I can help it,' he muttered.

'What was that? I didn't quite catch it.'

'I said, let me help you out. I might have some insights that will really help you win Andie over. Andrea, that is.'

'Really? Like what?' Wade asked eagerly.

'Well, do you talk shop with her?'

'Shop? You mean details about my business?' At Bruce's nod, Wade said, 'Not too much. I think most people are bored by accounting talk.'

'Most people, yes. But not Andie. She's an absolute financial groupie. Watches the money report every night on television — reads the *Wall Street Journal*. Why, she practically has the stock symbols on the *NASDAQ* memorized.'

'I didn't know that. I'd never have guessed.'

The poor dweeb looked so excited

Bruce almost felt sorry for him. He fell silent as the waiter served their drinks. After they were alone again, he made a big show of looking around to see if anyone was listening. Then he added in a low voice, 'To tell you the truth, she gets excited just talking about mutual funds.'

'No!'

'Yes!'

Wade sipped his sherry, then looked around before leaning closer to Bruce. 'Excited? You mean . . . excited as in — ?'

Bruce winked and nodded. 'Yeah, hot.' He waved his hand up and down. 'Scorching.'

A smile slowly broke over Wade's face. 'Maybe that's why I haven't been able to get to first base with her.'

Anger at the other man's comment as well as relief swept through Bruce. So Andie hadn't let him near her. Good for her, he thought. After tonight, she'd give him his walking papers for good.

'Mutual funds, huh?' Wade looked

around again then whispered, 'Any particular type of funds?'

Bruce was at a loss. His knowledge of mutual funds was limited to the ones he'd invested in. He thought hard trying to think of the most boring ones possible. 'Yeah, retirement funds.'

'No!'

'Yes, I swear! Just start whispering to her about retirement funds, and you won't know what hit you.'

'Well, that certainly puts a different spin on things. Maybe that's why she's kept me at arm's length. I just wasn't whispering the right kind of sweet nothings in her ear.'

Bruce felt a shaft of pure jealousy pierce him at the thought of Wade and Andie alone in the dark . . . with Wade whispering into her delectable ear.

* * *

In the powder room, Bruce's beautiful date wet a paper towel with cold water and handed it to Andie. 'Try pressing this to your throat. It should relax the muscles there.'

Andie took it from her with a quiet murmur of thanks. The cold compress did feel good. She looked up into the woman's eyes and started to speak, but the words died. Her eyes were just like Benton's.

'Who are you?' she gasped. Then she blushed. 'Sorry. Your eyes startled me. They look just like — '

'Bruce's?' The woman smiled.

When Andie nodded, she said, 'Everyone says that. I'm his sister, Darcy Whitaker.'

Andie felt weak with relief. 'His sister? You're Darcy? Why how nice to meet you.' So this was the sister who kept trying to fix him up.

Darcy Whitaker laughed. 'Well, it's nice to meet you too, even if the circumstances are rather strange. Odd that we should both be dining here tonight.'

'Yes, isn't it?' Andie knew it wasn't any coincidence that had brought them here tonight. That sneaky Benton had come here to spy on her. But why?

'So you're my brother's new partner? Bruce has talked about you — quite a bit, actually.'

'Really? I'm surprised.' Unable to resist, Andie filled Darcy in on how she and Benton had met. By the time she finished, Darcy was laughing so hard, she had to touch up her face again.

'That's the best story I've ever heard. My rough, tough brother — man-handled by a woman.'

'Guess that would make it woman-handled,' Andie said.

That set both of them off. They laughed together as if they were old friends. Andie dug into the tiny black evening bag for her compact.

'If only I had a picture of that scene I'd wrap it in silk, tie it with gold ribbon, and give it to my husband for his birthday. He'd pay any amount of money to see Bruce at the mercy of a woman.' She pulled a gold compact from her red beaded evening bag.

'Doesn't your husband like your brother?'

'Oh, he likes him fine. There's just been a little feud between them ever since Bruce caught Chase and me before we were married, one might say, in the act. Bruce has this rather old-fashioned feeling that his baby sister shouldn't have sexual thoughts.'

'With four brothers of my own, I know exactly what you're talking about.' Andic laughed. 'But isn't that a little hypocritical, considering his own reputation?'

'Oh, so you know about my brother, the playboy of the western world?'

'I got my information from a reliable source. Is it all true?'

'Well, he does seem to attract women, but you know, there hasn't been anyone in recent weeks. Chase — my husband — even commented on it.' She studied Andie. 'Hmm. He's not leading you astray, is he?'

Andie blushed. 'Oh, no. You don't have to worry about that. I make it a policy never to date cops. And he has no interest in me.'

'He doesn't?' Darcy asked, sounding doubtful.

'Not even a little bit. And I have none in him. Zero. Zilch. Nada.'

'Oh. Well, I'm kind of sorry to hear that. I like you. I think you'd be good for him.'

'Nope. No interest at all. I mean, we discussed it, but we agreed there's nothing there. Less than nothing.'

Darcy nodded. She started to speak, but Andie interrupted her. 'In fact, you might say we're totally neutral on that particular subject . . . '

She went on, talking nonstop about how uninterested she and Bruce were in each other, but Darcy was working too hard trying to hold in her laughter to listen. Andie Luft had it bad for her brother. Darcy had seen the signs too many times in his girlfriends not to know it.

The only thing she wondered was if Bruce felt the same about Andie.

Surprisingly, thinking back on the last couple of weeks, she decided he did. After all, he'd manipulated her into coming to dinner with him tonight, to the restaurant where Andie was dining with her date, and then had proceeded to go immediately to his new partner's side. Darcy couldn't wait to tell Chase about this startling turn of events.

A few minutes later, a woman from the wait staff entered the rest room and said, 'Excuse me, ladies, but your dates want to know if you're returning to the table.'

'Oh, my,' Darcy said. 'Have we been in here that long?'

She wiped her eyes and checked her reflection while Andie told the woman to please tell Bruce and Wade they'd be right out.

'I can't imagine what your brother has told my date,' Andie said with a grimace.

'What do you mean?'

'Well, no offense, Darcy, you're wonderful. I feel like we could be friends, but your brother has been rather difficult.'

'Difficult? My brother?' Darcy asked, trying not to laugh. For the first time in his life he'd met a woman who hadn't fallen at his feet. That in itself was challenging, but for that woman to be the one woman he wanted and couldn't get must be making him insane.

'Yes. I don't even want to tell you how rudely he's behaved.'

'I can't believe it,' Darcy said, playing devil's advocate. 'Bruce is the sweetest charmer any woman could ever meet. Why, he's got girls lining up to be with him. I think he majored in charm in college.'

'Well, you couldn't prove it by me,' Andie grumbled.

'Tell me, Andie, how serious are you about the guy waiting outside for you?'

'Wade?' She shrugged. 'I hate to say it, but I just don't think he's the man for me. I'm going to decline any future invitations from him.'

'Great! I mean, that's too bad, but

it's great because I know some single guys that would love to date you.'

'Oh, well, I don't know.'

'Hey, don't let your enthusiasm sweep you away,' Darcy joked.

'No, no, it's not that. It's just that . . . ' Andie made a face.

'Hey, I understand. Just tell me what you're looking for in a man, and I guarantee I can find you the perfect date,' Darcy said. What would happen if Bruce found out that she was fixing Andie up?

'I always thought I wanted a man in a safe career — not a cop like me — or like my dad.'

'I can understand that,' Darcy said, improvising. 'Who wants to talk shop with someone who lives the same kind of life? That would be pretty boring, I guess.'

'You know, I've always dated business types,' Andie confessed.

'Why?'

'Don't ask! It's a long story, and the men have already sent in one search party.'

Darcy reached into her tiny handbag and pulled out a card. 'Here's my phone number. Call me.' She giggled. 'Deal?'

Andie gave her a card in turn. 'If I don't call right away, you call me.'

Darcy followed Andie out of the restroom. Her head spun with ideas. She didn't know why Andie didn't realize that Bruce was hot for her. She suspected that Andie didn't even realize that she had the hots for Bruce. Those two definitely needed a helping hand. And she was the perfect person to help them. She could hardly wait to tell Chase.

★ ★ ★

Back at the table, the two men rose. Benton said, 'If it's all right with you, partner, why don't Darcy and I join you? I feel as if I've known Wade forever.'

'Great idea,' Wade said. 'That is, if you don't mind, Andrea?'

Benton grinned. To Andie's amazement, he winked at her. She blinked. 'Uh, yeah, sure. Darcy and I can finish our conversation.'

'Bite your tongue, Andie,' Darcy said with a giggle.

Wade held a chair for Darcy. He seemed stunned by her statuesque looks. 'Are you a model, Darcy?'

Her laughter rang out. 'Hardly.'

Andie looked at Benton and caught him looking back at her. His grin was definitely smug. The evening wasn't turning out at all like she'd planned. Resigned to the rather strange events that were unfolding, she sank onto the chair Benton held for her.

After he'd sat, Benton said, 'Wade was just telling me about some recent recommendations he's made to all his clients. Go ahead with your story, Wade.'

'Well, it's this new mutual fund.' He winked at Andie. 'This mutual fund combines elements of some of the safest stocks around — ranging from utility to bank stocks — but it seems to offer a rather healthy yield thus far.'

Wade droned on and on, repeating the phrase 'mutual funds' until Andie thought her eyes were glazing over. After a bit, Benton leaned close to her and whispered, 'Remember what I said?'

Andie remembered only too well.

'Mutual funds,' Benton whispered. 'Told you.'

9

Dismayed, Andie tried to think of a suitable reply, but before she came up with anything, Benton's pager began to beep.

'Sorry, forgot to put it on vibrate,' he said. Pushing away from the table, he unbuttoned his coat and silenced the pager clipped to his belt.

'Who is it?' Andie asked, figuring it was police business.

'I don't recognize the number.'

'May I see?' she asked.

With a grin, he handed her the pager.

'That's Ursula Lombardo's number,' she said, unable to keep the excitement out of her voice. She handed the pager back to him, then opened her handbag and removed her cell phone.

'Hand me your phone. I'll call her,' Benton said.

'No. I'll call her. That way if it's not

police-related I'll know immediately,' she said dryly.

Benton chuckled and agreed. Darcy asked Wade a question about mutual funds and soon had his full attention.

'Hi, Ursula, it's Sergeant Luft. What can I do for you?' After a couple of minutes, Andie said, 'No problem. I'll be right there.'

Relieved that she wouldn't have to be nice for the rest of the evening, Andie said, 'I'm sorry, Wade, but I have to go.'

'Why can't your partner take the call?' Wade asked, frowning.

'What Andie meant to say is that we both have to go,' Benton said, rising and pulling Andie's chair out.

'What about your sister?' Wade asked, sounding shocked that Benton planned to desert her.

'Hey, I'm used to this,' Darcy said, gathering her own purse and standing. 'That's why I always drive myself when Bruce asks me out.'

'Thanks, Stretch, I owe you,' Benton said.

'More than you know,' Darcy said, grinning back at him.

'I'll call you, Andrea,' Wade promised.

'Fine. You do that.' Fortunately, she didn't have to take his calls, Andie thought, exhilarated that she'd get to spend the evening with Benton instead of Wade.

★   ★   ★

When the parking valet pulled up in a classic Olds 442 convertible, Andie felt a shiver race up her spine. If she'd been asked to look through all the cars in the garage and pick the one she thought belonged to Benton, she'd immediately have chosen the lipstick-red car with the shiny mag wheels.

'Where's your truck?'

'At home. This is my date car.' He laughed at her awed expression.

The valet held the door for her. She slid onto the white leather upholstery seat with a sigh of pleasure. The huge

155

bucket seat felt as comfortable as her granddad's recliner. The car looked showroom perfect. 'You must keep this baby in a garage.'

'Yeah. I rent one at my apartment complex.' He grinned at her obvious admiration. 'Top up or down?' he asked, grasping the floor shifter.

'Leave it down,' Andie exclaimed, looking forward to feeling the wind in her face. As they pulled out from under the canopy, she asked, 'What year is this — '69?'

'Right. '69. Good guess.'

Andie laughed as she grabbed the silk velvet shawl to keep it from flapping. 'Don't sound so surprised. My dad adores old cars. He's got a '57 Chevy in one of the bays of our garage. He's been working on it for years.' She ran her hands over the white leather seat. 'He'd have a fit over this car.'

Accelerating, he moved to the inside lane of the feeder road and up the entrance ramp to the freeway.

'Wow, what pick-up,' Andie exclaimed.

'Have you got a standard 442 engine?'

He grinned. 'No. It's a Rocket 455.'

'I bet she'll fly,' Andie said, enviously. 'What'll she do?'

'Sergeant Luft, you sound as if you have a need for speed.'

'So sue me. I like fast cars. Don't most cops?'

'In a quarter mile, she'll do 98 in fifteen seconds,' he bragged.

'That's fast. You've got to bring her over and let my dad see her.'

'I'll do that,' he promised, glancing in the rearview mirror before he changed lanes.

Andie sat back and enjoyed the trip out to Universal City, while Benton told her how he'd bought the car when he'd been in high school. He'd finally restored it to its original beauty just last year.

'I'm surprised you take her out on the streets. I'd think you'd only take her to car shows.'

'A car's meant to be driven. What's the pleasure in just looking at one in your garage?'

'Yeah, I agree. I'd drive her, too. It must be pure pleasure.'

'You do understand, don't you?' He glanced over and his eyes caught hers.

The admiration she read there did funny things to her insides. Feeling suddenly shy, Andie looked away. After a minute, she told him the gist of her conversation with Ursula.

★ ★ ★

The drive didn't take nearly long enough, she thought as Benton turned onto Ursula's street. In the working-class neighborhood, most of the cars and pickups were parked in the driveways or on the street. Here, the one-car garages probably overflowed with the clutter of modern life.

'Park about a half a block away.' Andie pointed. 'Maybe in front of that pickup. We should be able to spot her brother immediately when he shows.'

'I have done this before,' Benton said, killing the engine. 'And you mean *if* he shows. Just because Ursula got a call from him doesn't mean he'll actually show up to beat the crap out of her for turning him in.'

The sudden quiet seemed unnatural. Andie's stomach suddenly growled.

'Hungry?' he asked.

'Yeah. I didn't even get an appetizer before your pager went off.'

'Open the glove compartment. There should be some pork rinds in there.'

'Ugh. Pork rinds? You eat pork rinds?'

'Hey, they're crispy and crunchy. They don't melt like candy, and they're filling. You never know when you might need a little something to tide you over.'

Andie did as he suggested and pulled out a plastic bag and tossed it to him.

When Benton ripped it open and offered her the bag, she said, 'No, thanks. They're disgusting. That's like eating lard. You might as well just pump cement into your arteries.'

'Whatever,' he said, grabbing a few and munching on them. 'Yum yum.' He licked the salt from his fingers.

Andie's stomach rumbled again. She hated to admit it, but she was so hungry even the atrocious pork rinds smelled good.

'Sure you won't have one?' he asked, holding the bag out again.

'Oh, all right. If you insist. I wouldn't want you thinking I'm a snob,' Andie said, grabbing a few. She nibbled. 'Hey, these aren't bad. Of course, anything tastes good if you're starving.'

Minutes turned into hours. They consumed every crumb of the pork rinds, then turned to quiet conversation. By midnight, the lights had been extinguished at the other houses. The light above the front door at Ursula's house shone like a beacon in the dark night.

Andie laid her head on the back of the seat and looked up at the stars. She yawned. 'These seats are too comfortable. You could practically make a bed here.'

'Use the lever on the side and lay it down. I'll wake you if anything develops.'

The thought tempted her, but she decided against it. Though she was drowsy, she didn't think she could drift to sleep with Benton's disturbing presence next to her.

'No, I'm fine. I'll just recline it a little so I can see the stars better. Did I tell you I had a telescope when I was in middle school?' She felt around with her right hand and found the lever. It dropped the seat back more than she wanted. She fiddled with it, trying to get it adjusted just right.

Suddenly, Benton crawled over the gearshift and flung himself atop Andie.

'What the — ' she muttered, pushing at him. 'Get off me!'

Benton raised up a little, though his body still pressed intimately against hers.

'Shhh,' he whispered. 'There's a guy walking down the sidewalk behind us.' He glanced backward quickly, then back down at her. 'White male — about six four. Ball cap.'

'That . . . doesn't . . . sound like

Lombardo,' she gasped, amazed she could speak at all. Feeling his body over hers seemed to turn her brain to mush. Or maybe it was the sudden pounding of blood through her veins — every drop of it making its way to the erogenous zones of her body. His action should have angered her, but it didn't. Instead, immense pleasure at his action — despite the reason — swept away any instinct to rebuff him. It was as if she'd unconsciously been waiting for this.

As she looked into Benton's eyes, she saw the pupils dilate. She quickly became aware of another change occurring in his body. A clichéd line from an old movie came to mind. She fought the urge to giggle and ask if that was a gun or was he just glad to see her.

'Must not be Lombardo,' he whispered. His voice was soft — and sensually rough.

'Guess not,' she whispered back. Her eyelids felt heavy. Involuntarily her hips lifted. A shudder racked his body. 'Benton?' She forced herself not to move again. She wanted him, but she was afraid of starting something she wouldn't be able to stop. He closed the distance between them until his mouth was a breath away from hers.

Andie didn't know what she expected, but the kiss that touched her lips was exactly what she wanted. She didn't hesitate, opening her mouth beneath his and welcoming his invasion. This time she didn't even try to suppress the moan of desire that welled from deep inside her. So much for good intentions, she thought.

The sound seemed to galvanize Benton. His kiss deepened, became frantic.

'Just what the hell do you kids think you're doing here?' an angry voice rasped.

Andie moaned — not from desire this time.

'It's okay,' he whispered, lifting his head.

Bruce stared at what was obviously an angry neighbor. It was the man in the ball cap. How could he have forgotten about the guy? How could he have forgotten about Lombardo? He felt like an idiot. He shielded Andie from view.

'Sorry, sir,' he said. His hands stroked Andie's shoulders where the straps of the dress had slid down, trying to convey to her that it was all right.

'Sorry won't cut it. And you're no kid. You're old enough to know better. This ain't no lovers' lane. I've already called the cops, so if you know what's good for you, you'll get on out of here.'

★ ★ ★

Bruce glanced at Andie from the corner of his eye. He'd tried to apologize. She'd listened, but then seemed madder than ever. She hadn't said a word on the trip back to town. He'd blown it. If she ever spoke to him again, he'd be surprised.

What had possessed him? Why had he let his hormones overrule his brain? He bit back a groan of frustration. He hadn't been able to help himself. Desire for her had finally overwhelmed his self-control. It was kiss her or die trying. Knowing Andie as well as he did now, he was surprised she hadn't punched him.

'Take the next right,' she said brusquely.

He complied, too upset over her coldness to notice the mansions lining the street. He'd really blown it. How could he have misunderstood her response? He'd been certain she was feeling the same thing as he. At least he'd wanted to believe she was.

If friendship was all he could have . . . He sighed and tried to smooth things over again. 'Look, Andie, I'm sorry. I wasn't really kissing you. It was the only thing I could think of to keep from blowing our cover.'

'How innovative of you,' she said in a voice that would have turned hot tamales to ice.

Bruce sighed. 'Which house?'

'That one.' She pointed to a two-story southern colonial complete with huge white columns and wraparound verandas on both floors.

Bruce pulled into the circular drive in front of the house and cut the engine. He started to get out, but Andie stopped him with a crisp, 'Don't bother. It's not like this was a date.'

'Right,' he said. He cleared his throat and tried for a casual tone as if she were no more important to him than any other cop. 'See you tomorrow, partner?'

Andie paused in pushing open the car door. For some reason, his farewell made her want to cry. She bit back the tears and said gruffly, 'Right. See you. Partner.'

She didn't wait to watch him drive away, but ran into the house as if something awful waited in the night to seize her. As soon as she'd slammed the front door, anger transformed to despair. A sob broke free from the suffocating pressure in her chest.

'Andie? Is that you?' her father called from his study.

Just what she needed. Quickly she

wiped the tears from her eyes, but she wasn't fast enough. Tom Luft had come out and stood at the foot of the stairs.

'Honey, what's wrong?'

She started to brazen it out, but she never had been able to fool him. Shoulders slumping, she sank onto a step. He climbed up to her. She put her arms around him and cried on his shoulder.

'Did Wade do something?' he asked. His quiet voice held an edge of anger.

'No. It's not Wade. I broke up with him.'

'Oh. Now I see why you're crying.'

'No. I'm crying because I'm just so — so — ' She swallowed a sob.

'I know, honey.' He patted her shoulder. 'It hurts even when it's you doing the breaking up.'

'I'm crying because I'm so mad I could scream!'

'What?' Her father sounded as bewildered as she felt.

'How can a man be so dense?'

'Uh, I don't know, honey. Which man are we talking about? Wade?'

'No, not Wade. How dare he say kissing me was part of the job.'

'What?' Tom Luft's forehead wrinkled in surprise.

'You know what he can do with his apologies?'

'Uh, I have a good idea,' he said cautiously, amusement glinting from his eyes.

'Thanks, Dad. You helped tremendously,' Andie said, kissing him on the cheek.

'Anytime,' he murmured.

When Andie left her father sitting on the step, he was scratching his head and looking bewildered.

All during the sleepless night, Andie told herself she should be happy that Benton wasn't attracted to her. She should be pleased that he accepted her as a cop, not a woman, but her hurt pride still smarted. All the rationalizations in the world wouldn't help her figure out how she was going to face him at work. He may not have kissed her with pleasure in mind, but she'd definitely felt desire for him — along with something even more unsettling — when she'd kissed him back.

How could they work together until this case was closed, now that she'd been in his arms? And getting back into his arms was the only thing she could think of. Andie punched her pillow because she knew she shouldn't even think along those lines.

Her only comfort was that she had a name for what ailed her. She wished it were just pure, old-fashioned lust — that was simple to cure. She punched her pillow again and wished it was Benton's hard head. What was she going to do? She was in love with her partner.

10

'It's going to take more than a cup of coffee to get me going this morning,' Andie muttered as Peyton filled her mug with inky black liquid.

'Don't tell me you and Benton are mad at each other again,' Peyton said, reaching for the powdered creamer.

'Okay, I won't tell you,' Andie said, preferring he think that's what was wrong with her.

'You two are something else. I thought you'd both adjusted pretty well to each other.'

'Actually, we have. He doesn't try to give me all the boring jobs, and I don't force them back on him.'

'So what's the problem?'

'Nothing, Peyton. I'm just tired this morning. Late night.' Andie saw a couple of the other men coming toward them. She didn't want any talk to get started about a romance between her and Benton. She quickly added sugar and creamer to her coffee. Maybe it would taste better than it smelled. 'Got to go, Peyton.'

'Be careful out there, Andie.'

She smiled her thanks at him and hurried away. He knew Benton too well — and her. She hoped he didn't suspect anything.

The kiss Benton had given her had been the kind of kiss heroines in romance novels received. Andie touched her index finger to her lips. Just thinking about his mouth on hers made her lips tingle. If Benton had come over right now, grabbed her, and laid another one on her, she'd have taken it and given thirty minutes to draw a crowd.

Had he really been protecting their cover? Or was he interested in her? There was no mistaking the way his body had reacted. But was that just a male response he had no control over? Would he have reacted that way to any woman?

Those questions haunted Andie. Unfortunately, she'd never cared enough about any man to wonder about such matters. If only she had someone she could ask. Her four older brothers had always been the ones she turned to with questions — they'd been her best friends growing up — but she couldn't imagine asking any of them to explain Benton's behavior. She didn't even want to think of how far off the deep end they'd jump after a question like that.

Andie sank onto her chair with a tired sigh. The more she thought about last night, the more confused she became. The best course of action was to forget it, she decided.

'So what do you think about my plan?' Benton asked from the desk next to hers.

He hadn't mentioned the kiss. The only thing he'd said was that Ursula had probably laughed her head off over the wild goose chase she'd sent them on. As for Ursula, she'd called Benton this morning and said she'd left her house and checked into a hotel right after she'd paged him.

'I disagree with it,' Andie said, determined to never think of that kiss again. From this moment on, it would be business as usual. After all, he was a cop. She didn't date cops, she reminded herself. End of story.

'You would.' Benton grinned at her.

Something inside her brightened. She grinned back. 'That's right. I would because I have a brain in my head.' She watched as he rolled his gorgeous silver eyes.

He gulped some of the repulsive black liquid they called coffee and scowled. 'So what do you think we should do, Nancy Drew?'

There was one problem with her policy of not falling for a cop: it couldn't undo something that had already happened, she realized. Her heart sank.

'Don't call me that,' she said, feeling a bit like crying.

With a chuckle, he said, 'Okay, cupcake.'

'Definitely don't call me that!' She swallowed the knot of emotion and concentrated on her coffee as if it held the answer to her problems.

'Come on, Luft. Time to get going.' Benton pushed away from his desk and stood, stretching his arms overhead.

He looked so damn enticing, she had to look away. The plain white T-shirt he wore emphasized his muscular build. He'd paired it with his usual faded jeans, which made him look so good she wanted to strip them from him. He slipped on his sport coat to conceal the shoulder holster he wore. His fingers raked through his straight black hair before he donned a ball cap.

'Move it. We've got things to do and places to go.'

Andie groaned, more from frustrated desire than anything. 'You know it's going to be over a hundred again today.'

'Oh, don't tell me a little thing like a heat wave is going to stop one of San Antone's finest from doing her sworn duty?'

'Up yours, Benton,' she said crossly as she gathered her shoulder bag and followed him to the T-Bird.

Down in the garage, she pretended to fight for the chance to drive again today, but she was glad when he beat her to it. Last night had taken a toll on her, and she was simply too tired to deal with traffic. Let Benton handle it, she thought, grateful just to lean her head against the ugly vinyl seat and close her eyes, hiding behind the reflective sunglass lenses.

A half hour later, Benton slid the gearshift into park but didn't automatically cut the engine. He let it idle with the air-conditioning on while he looked at his partner.

Andie had fallen asleep a while ago. She'd slept soundly, as he made an endless series of turns to get to this wedding chapel, sliding around on the slick vinyl seat until she'd ended up against him with her head on his shoulder.

The denim skirt she wore — some

175

kind of wraparound thing that tied at her waist — had slid up her long legs, revealing a golden swath of skin he longed to kiss. Today she wore red sneakers and a red T-shirt. She'd had red lipstick on when she'd come to work, but it had worn off on the coffee cup before they'd left. Now, her lips were nearly free of lipstick. He imagined kissing her again — right now. This minute. Just the thought made him so hard he groaned. If thinking about kissing her made him ready to explode, he didn't know what he'd do if he ever got close to her again.

Bruce reached out and brushed a blond curl off her cheek, tucking it behind her ear. She stirred. He quickly removed his hand. He didn't want to risk their relationship again, especially since she seemed to have dismissed last night's incident. He gently shoved her over to her side of the seat and tilted her head to rest against the car door.

'Wake up,' he said, purposely making his voice gruff. 'We're here.'

Instantly, she straightened. He could imagine those big green eyes blinking rapidly as she tried to look alert.

'I know we're here,' she said, opening her door. 'You don't have to announce the obvious.' Andie reached up with her index finger and pushed the mirrored sunglasses down on the bridge of her nose so she could fix Benton with a gimlet stare.

A shaft of pain hit her as she turned to stare at a wedding chapel. This one was a quaint, white frame bungalow, probably built in the nineteen-fifties. Marigolds and petunias filled the flowerbeds that skirted the house, and asparagus fern overflowed two white planters on either side of the front door.

She imagined walking down the aisle and tried to imagine who would be waiting for her at the altar. Suddenly, she could see Benton standing there in a black tux, looking handsome, laughter dancing in his eyes as he reached for her hand.

A sign that said to please come in

kept her from ringing the bell. An electronic beep sounded as they stepped in, and an elderly woman opened the door at the other end of the room. 'Oh, hello, you lovebirds,' she chirped. 'You've come to the right place to have a memorable ceremony.'

'No, ma'am.' Andie paled at the longing that hit her. 'That's not why we're here.'

'Oh.' The woman's expression went from joyous to sad in a split second. 'I'm so disappointed.' She looked over at Benton and whispered to Andie, 'What's the matter, dearie? Is he afraid of commitment? So many young men these days — '

Before Andie could speak, Benton said, 'It's not me, ma'am. It's her.'

Andie froze him with a look. 'What my partner's trying to say, ma'am, is that we're here on business.'

'Yes, ma'am, all joking aside. We need to ask you a few questions.' Benton flashed his identification and so did Andie. 'You are Mrs. Nora Hubbard?'

At her nod, he said, 'You and your husband John operate this chapel?'

'That's right, but I'm afraid I don't understand why you want to talk with me,' Mrs. Hubbard said.

'We understand Pippo Lombardo has freelanced for your chapel when you want to provide photography services,' Andie said.

'Oh, Pippo!' the woman said. 'Yes, that's right. He's such a dear boy.'

'Dear boy?' Andie echoed, sounding doubtful.

'Why, yes! We were having trouble with one of our cars — it's actually my old Cadillac. Pippo volunteered last month to take it to a mechanic friend. He told us his friend would repair it if we just paid for the cost of the parts.'

'Who is it, Nora?' a tall, stooped man called from the doorway.

'It's this nice young couple, dear. They're asking some questions about Pippo.'

'Well, the teakettle is boiling. Ask them to come back to the kitchen.'

'Oh, yes. That's a great idea. Why don't you two kids follow me? John and I always have a cup of tea this time of the morning and a piece of wedding cake.'

'Wedding cake?'

'Yes, I guess it's what you call an occupational hazard. We always have leftover wedding cake in the fridge.'

She turned, despite their refusal to share her snack. Andie sighed and followed.

'So do you two kids want a cup of coffee or some tea?' the man asked, holding the steaming kettle in his hand while his wife withdrew two more cups from the cupboard.

They both declined, but sat at the table while the elderly couple had their snack.

'About this car you loaned Lombardo,' Benton said. 'Could you give me the license plate number and a description?'

The woman looked confused. 'Why would you want that information?'

'We have reason to believe Lombardo is involved in a series of thefts,' Andie said. 'His car hasn't been seen in weeks. Chances are he's using another one — probably yours. We'd like to report it as a stolen car.'

'Oh, no. He's called every week with a progress report on it. His friend is just having a hard time getting parts for it. I can't believe Pippo is a thief,' Mrs. Hubbard said defensively.

Her husband covered her blue-veined hand with his and said, 'Nora, I was just thinking about that ring of your mother's that went missing a few months ago.'

'Her garnet dinner ring?'

He nodded. 'You discovered it was gone a few days after Pippo visited.'

'Surely he wouldn't steal from us.' She raised watery eyes to Andie. 'Would he?'

Andie felt sorry for the woman. Gently, she said, 'I'm afraid we can answer that only if we locate him.'

The woman pushed her cake away. 'We've been good to Pippo and have always given him good referrals. Other events need photographers — not just weddings.'

Benton took over the questioning, writing down a description of the car and its license plate. Unfortunately, the Hubbards didn't have any more information to offer. He didn't tell the elderly couple that they'd probably never see their car again. He and Andie both knew the old Cadillac was already south of the border. Lombardo had most likely bought another vehicle by now with the money from selling the classic car.

Angered, Andie suddenly had an inspiration. 'Benton, what about your sister's fashion show?'

He snapped his fingers. 'Luft, you're brilliant.'

She glowed at his compliment. 'Mrs. Hubbard,' she said. 'If Pippo does call again, we'd like you to tell him about a charity fashion show coming up this Saturday. The organizers are still looking for a photographer.' She turned to Benton. 'What phone number can we give him?'

Benton thought and wrote one down. 'This is Darcy's pager number, through Sunbelt Oil. If they have to issue her another, it's no problem.' To the Hubbards, he said, 'Tell Lombardo their contracted photographer canceled and they're desperate. They'll pay whatever he asks.'

They each gave their cards to the Hubbards. 'If you do hear from him, call us,' Benton said. He and Andie thanked them and left.

As soon as they got on the road, Andie called in the information on the Hubbards' car. 'Maybe we'll get lucky and someone will spot the tags.'

'You and I both know he's smart enough to switch the tags and spray the car a different color. Anyway, chances are it's in Mexico.'

'Poor Nora. She'll probably never get her mother's ring back,' Andie said. 'If Lombardo does call, do you think he'll fall for this?'

'It's a long shot, but, hell, maybe. I have a feeling he's like most perps — greedy enough to be stupid sooner or later.'

'Lucky for us it's not like in the movies,' Andie said.

Benton laughed. 'Yeah, I haven't met a rocket scientist yet.'

★ ★ ★

The sun was sinking low when Andie pulled into the garage at home, tired and discouraged. Her footsteps dragged as she stepped inside the kitchen. The house was silent. It was rare that Tom Luft came home before eight in the evening. Her father was still the workaholic he'd always been. Her granddad was off playing poker with some other retired military friends. With all her brothers assigned to different parts of the United States, it was seldom they were all home at the same time. More and more, she seemed to come home to an empty house. Suddenly she missed her family intensely.

After she'd changed into khaki shorts, sneakers, and a tank top, she grabbed an apple from the fridge and headed to the den. Munching on the tart Granny Smith apple, she flipped channels to see if there was anything worth watching on television.

Just as she'd decided there wasn't, the phone rang. She picked it up and before she could even say hello, she heard Benton say, 'Luft, officer needs assistance.' He sounded frantic.

'What is it?'

'It's Sophie. I'm over at my sister's house, babysitting, and I can't get her to stop crying.'

Andie frowned. 'What can I do?'

'Get over here and tell me if she needs to go to the ER,' he exclaimed.

'Calm down. I'm sure she's just fine.' Because he sounded so panicked, Andie agreed to come. She jotted down directions, smiling at the thought of this big guy being so scared over a small child. She exchanged her shorts for slacks and her sneakers for a pair of boots. Then she covered her tank top with a white cotton camp shirt, and she was ready to leave.

A half hour later, she pulled into the drive of a rockfaced home in the estate section of one of San Antonio's newest subdivisions. Before she could ring the bell, the front door flew open. Benton hadn't been lying. The little girl was crying at the top of her lungs.

'What's wrong with her?' he asked, looking and sounding as upset as the child.

'I don't know,' she said, stepping in and closing the door behind her. She dropped her handbag on the antique console table in the foyer.

'What do you mean you don't know? You're a woman.'

Amused, Andie said, 'What's that got to do with anything?'

'Well,' he floundered, 'women are mothers. They know things.'

'This woman isn't a mother yet, so I don't know any more than you. Let me see her.'

'Sophie doesn't go to strangers,' Benton said.

When Andie held out her arms, the tearful little girl reached for her.

'Well, I'll be — '

Andie interrupted, 'Watch your language.' She bounced the child up and down. 'She doesn't feel wet. Are you thirsty, Sophie?' The child didn't reply, but her crying subsided a little as she stared at Andie with big blue eyes.

Andie walked into the great room, still bouncing the baby gently and rubbing her back. She kept this up for a while, but Sophie still cried. She handed her back to Benton. 'Let me call my dad. He was mother and father to all of us after my mom died. He'll know what to do.'

Benton bounced Sophie while Andie tried to get him on the phone. When Tom Luft answered, she explained the situation. After a couple of minutes, she said, 'He wants to know how long she's been like this?'

'Since about a half hour after I fed her tonight.'

She relayed the information, then asked what he'd fed her.

Benton looked stricken. 'Oh.'

'Oh, what?'

'Darcy had fixed some steamed carrots and stuff for her. I was eating some leftover burritos their cook fixed yesterday.'

Andie stared. 'You didn't?'

'She wouldn't eat the carrots,' he said defensively.

Andie laughed. 'Never mind, Dad. I think we have the answer to Sophie's problem. Benton fed her some bean burrito.'

After Andie had hung up, Benton said, 'Well, I mushed it up. Beans are the in thing — high fiber, protein, all that stuff. I didn't think it would hurt.'

'I think Sophie has a case of gas,' Andie said. 'Poor little thing,' she crooned. She began to rub the child's tummy in a circular motion, which seemed to quiet her.

They sat together on the couch. Andie placed Sophie on her tummy across her lap. 'Dad said to just let her lay like this and rub her back. He said Mom used to do this with the boys, because they all had colic when they were babies and this seemed to be the only thing that helped.'

'I'll put some music on. Darcy always has that easy-listening stuff on her CD player. Maybe that'll help.'

Andie watched him as he crossed the room and turned on the stereo. The mellow sound of Kenny G filled the room. When he returned to the couch and sat next to her, she realized Sophie had stopped crying and just sniffled now.

'Looks like she might fall asleep,' Benton whispered.

Andie looked at him, inches away, and could only nod. The music filled the room, and Benton filled her senses. For an hour, they listened to music that must have been selected for one purpose and one purpose only: seduction. After Kenny G, an album of love songs from the eighties played.

She leaned her head back against the couch and imagined herself and Benton, alone in the room with the lights turned low. She didn't know if she was grateful or disappointed that little Sophie was with them.

11

'How old were you when your mother died?' Benton suddenly asked.

'Ten. I'll never forget that night when Dad woke me to tell me. I'd never seen him cry before.'

'What happened?'

'Mom had been coming back from a night class at the college. A drunk driver hit her.'

'Your dad was a cop then, wasn't he?'

'Yes. Mom hated his job. I can remember her crying whenever an officer was killed in action. They argued about it. She begged him to do something else, but he loved being a cop. After she died, he left the force because he had five kids to raise and couldn't do it with the hours he worked.' Andie blinked rapidly. 'If only he'd done it before.'

Benton reached over and caught a

lone tear on the tip of his finger. Now he understood her reluctance to date cops. She was acting on the bitterness of a ten-year-old, but he doubted she understood that.

'Your dad loved being a cop, just like you?'

She nodded.

'Do you think it's right for someone who loves you to ask you to stop doing the job you love because it frightens them?'

Andie stared at him. He easily read the anger in her expression. Before she could defend her mother's position, her pager beeped, waking Sophie up. Andie began rubbing the toddler's back again. 'My pager's in my purse. Can you get it?'

He hurried to the foyer and grabbed her purse, opened it and silenced the pager. With a groan, he said, 'It's Ursula again.'

He grabbed the phone and called their would-be snitch.

'What's this? Another wild goose

chase?' he asked.

He listened and then sighed. 'Okay. Go on to the hotel and leave the back gate open. We'll be there by midnight.' He hung up. 'You don't have to go if you don't want to,' he said.

Andie thought about it. If she had any brains, she would not return to the scene of the crime, so to speak.

Sophie stirred, then stretched and rolled over, blinking sleepy blue eyes at Andie.

'Hi, Sophie,' Andie said. 'Tummy feel better?'

The little girl nodded. 'Where's Unca Boo?'

Andie smiled. 'Unca Boo's right over there.'

Benton sat next to her again and his niece went tumbling into his arms.

When Benton's arms tightened around the tiny child and he kissed her gently on the cheek, something inside Andie melted.

She was thankful she heard voices in the kitchen before she got completely mushy and tearful to boot.

'Mommy and Daddy are home,' Benton told Sophie.

When Darcy and her husband came in, their laughter changed to anxiety when they saw Sophie.

'Why's she still up? Is she sick? Does she have a fever?'

'Relax, relax,' Benton reassured his sister as he handed Sophie to her. The little girl snuggled against Darcy's neck.

'Chase, this is my partner, Andie Luft,' Benton said.

Chase smiled and nodded, but his attention was on his daughter.

'Sophie had a little stomachache,' Benton confessed. When he told Darcy and Chase what he'd fed her, Darcy shook her finger at him and told him with mock severity that he'd better never do that again. By this time, Sophie was giggling as her father tickled her.

They chatted a few minutes more. Lombardo still hadn't contacted Darcy. Benton assured Chase again that there would be no danger to Darcy or anyone if Lombardo did arrange to come to the fashion show. The Whitakers walked them to the door.

Outside, Andie asked, 'Your truck or my car?'

Benton looked at her small sports car. 'No offense, Luft, but I don't feel like folding myself into that thing. I don't know how you manage it.'

'Pick me up at my house then.' Andie drove quickly home. Excitement hummed in her. She told herself it was just because they had another chance to pick up Lombardo.

Benton pulled in behind her. She tossed her handbag on the seat and climbed up into the roomy truck. On the way to Ursula's house, he surprised her by asking, 'Tell me, Luft, do you plan to marry? Or are you just playing cop until then?'

'Yes, I'd like to marry someday. And no, I'm not just filling my days by playing cop. I really like being a cop. Well, most of the time I do. It's some of the people in the department I don't like.'

'Like Aiello?' he asked with a grin.

She agreed. 'You never told me what you did to get on the esteemed lieutenant's bad side.'

Benton grinned. 'You show me yours and I'll show you mine — so to speak.'

Andie flushed. 'Do you have to make everything sound sexual?'

'Yes.'

Surprised, Andie laughed. 'Okay, you win. I'll go first.' Benton was too appealing by far. 'When I first joined the force, Aiello was my lieutenant. From day one, he'd make excuses to talk to me — brush up against me.'

'Why, that — ' Benton clamped his mouth shut. 'What did you do?'

'It was always in a way that made me uncertain whether he did it intentionally or not.' She grimaced. 'This isn't exactly an original story. Finally, one night, he made an overt play for me — grabbed my — well, you get the picture. I decked him. End of story.'

Andie looked over. Benton looked murderous but all he said was, 'You decked him? I'd have given anything to see that. Did you break any bones?' he asked, sounding hopeful.

'You're terrible,' Andie said, chuckling. 'Unfortunately, he denied he was trying anything, and he filed a complaint against me. Then, my dad joined the fight without my knowledge. I don't know what he did, but Aiello backed down and withdrew his complaint. Ever since, though, he's given me a hard time. When I joined Robbery, I thought I'd get away from him. Then they decentralized Robbery so I ended up stuck at the substation with him.'

'You could ask for a transfer,' Bruce said, angered that she'd had to put up with that sort of thing.

'Yes, but I get a perverse pleasure out of seeing the veins in his forehead stand out when he has to deal with me.' She nodded at him. 'Your turn now.'

'Oh, nothing as dramatic as that. But it did involve a woman I was dating.'

'Of course,' Andie said dryly.

Benton grinned. 'Turns out he had designs on her, too. She'd dated him first, which I didn't know. So the way he read it, she dumped him for me, and the feud was on.'

'Well, he certainly can carry a grudge,' Andie said. 'He gives new meaning to the old saying, don't get mad, get even. Why did he think you'd be furious at having to partner with me?'

Bruce shrugged. 'The woman involved then was another cop. She was into a power play. I had such a bad experience with her, I swore I'd never have another woman partner.'

'I see. Sorry you were forced into it.'

'No problem. At least you're a good cop. She wasn't.'

Andie warmed beneath his praise. 'Thanks, Benton. By the way, what happened to the woman?'

He grinned. 'She ended up going back to Aiello after we broke up. She married the jerk.'

Andie's mouth dropped in shock.

'So I always make a point to tell him to give my regards to his wife.'

Andie burst into laughter. 'I bet that really makes those veins in his forehead pop. That's awful.' She tried not to feel jealous about a past relationship he'd had, but it was difficult.

Benton killed the headlights and coasted to a stop a block away from Ursula's house.

'Just in case Ursula's up to something, you go in through the back gate. I'll take the front door as she suggested.'

'Okay. Hope you have a padlock on your zipper in case she has something else on her mind,' Andie joked.

'Hm. You're not jealous, are you?'

Was it her imagination or did he sound hopeful? 'Not in the slightest,' she said, removing the small AMT .380 from her purse and tucking it in her boot. She shoved her purse under the seat.

'I like your toy,' Benton said,

unlocking the glove compartment and removing his own gun and holster. 'Watch your back.'

'Yeah. You watch your front,' she muttered as she followed him, ducking between the cars parked along the street until they were one house away from their goal. She and Benton separated at the neighbor's garage. Bruce approached the front door while she dashed to the ramshackle privacy fence that enclosed Ursula's hard-scrabble yard. She slipped the latch on the gate.

The moon ducked behind a cloud and made the backyard dim and murky. Andie flattened herself against the back wall of the house. She placed her feet carefully, not wanting to trip over a rake or something left in the yard. Although judging by the weed-choked flower beds, garden implements weren't likely to be a threat.

Andie peeked around the corner and saw a small concrete slab patio and the back door. She stepped out carefully, but didn't see anything amiss. Just then something stirred in the shadows on the patio. Andie froze, heart pounding. The moon came out from the cloud and spotlighted the patio. Andie gulped. The something that moved was Ralph the pit bull.

Oh, hell! The dog must have caught her scent or seen her. He started alternately growling and barking like there was no tomorrow. Andie knew not to run because he'd be on her in a flash. Her brain froze. Ralph began walking toward her.

'Good dog,' she said, her voice sounding as shaky as she felt. She took a careful step backwards. The dog took two steps forward. Andie took another step backwards. Ralph advanced.

He probably weighed nearly as much as she, Andie thought, feeling behind her for the corner of the house. Maybe she could duck around the corner, then run like hell for the gate.

Just then the back door flew open and Benton stepped out.

'Yo, Ralph,' he said, his voice stern.

The dog froze. Though he swung his head at Benton, his body remained facing Andie. She didn't hesitate. The corner of the house was just a blur as she dashed for the gate.

'Ralph, sit!' she heard Benton thunder. But the dog didn't listen. She heard him coming.

'Run, Andie!' Benton yelled from behind.

She made it with a second to spare. She slammed the rickety gate and leaned her weight against it. The dog hit the gate like a battering ram. She heard Benton cursing and knew he was trapped in the yard with the dog.

Desperately, she scrambled for her gun in her boot, not wanting to kill the animal, but hoping if she shot into the air, the sound would scare it away. Her hands trembled as she jerked the gate open just in time to see Ralph running full speed at Benton.

With her heart in her throat, she yelled, 'Ralph. Here! Here, boy!' Ralph skidded to a stop and turned. Then he charged her. Benton scrambled over the side fence. Andie slammed the gate again and didn't wait for the vicious dog to slam against it this time. She shoved her gun back in her boot and ran to the neighbor's backyard, hoping there was no canine monster in it, too.

Benton met her halfway. She threw her arms around him and clung as relief made her knees weak.

'You all right?' he asked breathlessly. She could only nod. Finally, she gasped, 'You?'

'Yeah, I'm fine. We better get out of here. Lights are coming on all over the place.'

He hurried her to the front and they ducked behind a panel van parked on the street. Silently he comforted her until her trembling stopped.

'Let's go home,' he said, guiding her back to his truck.

A short while later he pulled into an apartment complex, parked and walked around to open her door.

Dazed, she looked around. 'Where are we?'

'My place. Come on. You look too shook up to go home just yet.'

She didn't complain when he put his arm around her waist and guided her to the stairs.

In his apartment, he started to turn on the lights but she stopped him.

'All right,' he said. 'Coffee or something stronger?'

She shuddered. 'I don't think I can swallow anything.'

'Go sit down. You need something with sugar.'

Andie didn't argue. Dully, she looked around the room. Moonlight shining in through the patio doors illuminated the room. She walked over to the huge leather sofa and collapsed. She removed her gun from her boot and kicked her boots off. Curling into a ball on the sofa, she just wanted to hide.

Benton wouldn't want anything to do with her after this. Some partner she'd been.

'Here, drink this.'

She heard ice clink and took the glass

he'd given her. To her surprise, it was lemonade. Even more surprising, she found she was thirsty. The drink helped refresh her.

'I'm sorry, Benton.'

'Sorry? About what?' he asked, shrugging out of the shoulder holster and laying it on the coffee table next to her backup weapon.

'I let you down.' She set the glass on the coffee table and covered her face with both hands. To her horror, she burst into tears

'Hey, Luft, it's okay.'

When she didn't respond, Benton moved closer. 'Andie, you did good.'

She shook her head.

'Yes, you did. In the face of something completely terrifying to you, you didn't panic. In fact, you came back to help me. A cop can't ask any more of his partner than that.'

Andie wiped her eyes and looked at him. He was very close. 'Do you mean that?'

'Hey, would I lie to you?'

Andie gave him a shaky smile. 'You're not going to tell the other guys about this?'

When he shook his head, she asked, 'Cross your heart?'

Solemnly, he crossed his heart and added, 'And hope to die.'

A chill shook Andie at his words. Impulsively, she reached out and pressed her fingertips against his lips. 'Don't say that, Bruce. Don't ever say that.'

At her touch, his teasing grin faded. His heart began to beat like a trip hammer. He lifted her fingers from his mouth and held her hand. 'Andie, you called me Bruce.'

Without breaking eye contact, Bruce lifted her hand to his lips again and tenderly kissed each finger. He felt the shudder that racked Andie's body. With a groan, he pulled her into his arms. Their lips met, and he was lost.

In a frenzy, he kissed her as if he were making up for all the times he'd wanted to and couldn't.

Andie matched him kiss for kiss. When he tugged her T-shirt free from her jeans, she didn't protest. Instead, she held her arms up so he could remove it. Then she repeated the action with him. When she reached behind for the clasp of her bra, he stopped her with a kiss.

'Let me,' he whispered. He kissed his way down her throat, glorying in the soft sounds she made and in the way her hands gripped his head and held him close.

Part of him wanted to take her — bond with her in the most primitive way, but another part of him, a part he hadn't known existed, wanted to prolong this, draw it out, give her the kind of pleasure she'd never forget.

When he reached behind her and unclasped her bra, his hands shook. Her skin branded him as he brushed the bit of white lace aside. Andie arched into him. 'You're killing me,' she moaned.

He drew back from her. 'Am I hurting you?'

'Yes, with tenderness.' Andie flattened her hands on his chest and pushed. Bruce fell back against the cushions. Andie reached for the button of his jeans and unfastened it.

He thought he'd never see anything that excited him more than her above him, perfect breasts revealed by the moonlight. When she encircled his neck with her arms and lay against him as she sought his lips, he went rigid. The feeling of her breasts against him nearly undermined what little control he had left.

'Andie, stop,' he whispered. 'I can't take it.'

She froze, looking uncertain. Bruce levered himself up, then gathered her into his arms and carried her to the bedroom.

'We're going to make love in bed. Like lovers,' he said as he stood her next to the bed. He swept aside the covers on his bed, then finished undressing her with reverent hands, kissing each part of her he uncovered.

Andie shivered with each kiss. When she bestowed the same favors on him, he understood how she felt.

'Be gentle,' he whispered when she removed his briefs.

Laughter bubbled from her. 'I'll try,' she whispered, sitting on the edge of the bed, then sliding to the middle. She held out her arms. 'Come to me, love,' she whispered.

Andie saw his grin fade as he covered her. His maleness demanded entrance, and she welcomed him with joy. His body branded hers with heat. His kiss was fierce and demanding. She answered his demands with her own.

Her hips moved against him in a dance as old as time itself. Andie wanted it to last forever, yet she rushed headlong toward the precipice, unable to stand the exquisite tension that gripped her body and soul. With a cry, she slipped over the edge and tumbled into paradise. Faintly, she heard Bruce's hoarse sound of satisfaction as he joined her. She gripped his back, holding him to her as he poured himself into her — holding him as if she'd never let him go.

Sleep came swiftly. Sometime before dawn she felt his hands on her. Smiling drowsily, she welcomed his kisses. This time their joining was gentle and slow, but the end result was the same meeting of souls.

She was almost asleep, with Bruce inside her, when she heard him whisper, 'I love you, Andie.'

12

Bruce pulled into Andie's driveway just as the sun came up.

'You can't pretend last night didn't happen,' he finally said.

Andie wouldn't look at him. 'I'll see you at the office in a bit.'

His temper was ragged and had been that way since he'd awakened to find himself alone in bed. Andie, dressed in her rumpled clothes, was in his kitchen brewing coffee when he'd walked in with a towel wrapped around his waist. She'd quickly looked away and asked him to take her home as soon as he was dressed. That was the beginning of the end.

'If I did something wrong, at least tell me what it was.'

Andie opened the door hurriedly and climbed out.

'Andie!' The hurt in his voice must

have stopped her.

Slowly, she turned and looked at him. 'You said you love me,' she whispered.

'And that's wrong?'

'You can't love me. I can't love you. I shouldn't have let myself get carried away last night.'

'Andie, you wouldn't have done that if you didn't care. You love me too. I know you do, whether you'll admit it or not.'

'Oh, Bruce, just go. Please.'

'Grow up, Andie. You're not ten years old. I'm not your father and you're not your mother.'

Angry, she slammed the door and hurried inside.

Her grandfather and her dad sat in the kitchen, drinking coffee. They both looked up, looked her over, then hurriedly looked down at their cups.

Andie lifted her head and walked past them. Then she raced up the stairs and slammed the door of her room.

By the time she'd finished showering,

hating to wash the scent of their lovemaking from her body, she'd cried her last tear. Somehow, she'd have to go to work, be with Bruce, and not let anyone suspect that her heart was breaking.

Later at HQ she tried her best to act normally, but it was a strain. Bruce wouldn't even look at her. That was best. And that was what she wanted, she thought. Then why did it hurt so much?

By the time Darcy Whitaker called, Andie was falling apart. Bruce took notes fast, listening rather than speaking. He said goodbye, then hung up.

'It looks like we might finally manage to close this case,' Bruce said. 'Darcy says Pippo took the bait. He'll be there.'

'That's good,' Andie said. 'Ursula's been a wash. I've never met such a nervous Nellie.'

'Yeah, she could have told us she was leaving that damned dog in the backyard last night,' he complained.

Poor Bruce. He looked as bad as she

felt. Peyton and Luis had been ribbing him all morning about the bags under his eyes.

In two days, they'd close this case; she felt it in her bones. Then she could go back to her regular job, and Bruce to his. She'd never have to see him again. Which was undoubtedly why she felt so miserable.

'We need to talk,' Benton said in a low voice after he'd finished briefing Luis and Peyton about the fashion show Saturday.

'There's nothing to talk about,' Andie said in an anguished whisper.

'Like hell there's not. Have you thought about the consequences of what we did last night?'

She'd thought of little else. 'Get over it, Benton,' she blustered, trying to make him back off. 'It was just sex.'

He looked offended which was what she wanted. 'Just sex? Is that all it was to you?'

Andie settled for a shrug.

His lips tightened. He looked as hurt

as if she'd yanked his heart out of his body and trampled on it. 'Even if it was nothing but sex, you might think about the fact that we made love twice — without protection. What about that?'

The importance of what he was trying to say dawned on her. She felt the blood rush to her face. She hadn't thought about the consequences of her actions. Now that she did, the thought of possibly having made a baby with the man she loved sent a rush of pleasure straight to her soul. Unfortunately, she knew there was little chance that had happened.

To him, she whispered, 'You don't have to worry. It's probably not the right time of the month.' When she glanced over at him, she was taken aback by how disappointed he looked.

'Andie, we have to talk. This whispering back and forth is ridiculous. Let's go someplace where we can talk.'

'Oh, no.'

'You can trust me. I won't do

anything you don't want me to do,' he promised.

When she didn't reply, just stared at him with such stark longing, he laughed softly. 'I see. It's not me you're worried about.' Then he said in a voice of such tenderness that her resolve wavered, 'Come on, love. I'm yours. Do with me as you will.' His eyes were hot as he lowered his gaze to her breasts. Andie burned as if he'd touched her there.

'Stop it,' she hissed, mortified.

'Then promise me you'll meet me tonight,' Bruce said simply.

Andie looked around, suddenly aware that a lot of the guys seemed to be looking their way.

'I promise. I promise.'

The day dragged as she and Bruce made plans for catching Lombardo at the fashion show.

Eventually, to Andie's relief, it was time to go home. When she finally pulled in, she was shocked to see all her brothers shooting hoops in the drive-way.

They surrounded her car. Jack, the oldest, opened her car door and Evan and Greg, the twins, pulled her out. Mike, the one closest to her in age, ruffled her hair. 'Hey, Squirt. About time you got home.'

'What are you guys doing here?' Andie asked, hugging and kissing each of them, genuinely glad to see them.

'We kind of missed the old homestead,' Jack said, bouncing the basketball.

'Yeah, Greg and I were talking with Jack the other day. He mentioned he was coming home so we thought we'd take a few days and come too.'

'You mean the FBI can get along without the Texas twins?' Andie teased.

'I figured if the NSA can let Jack loose, then the Bureau could manage without us for a few days,' Evan said.

'Same here,' Mike huffed, wiping perspiration from his forehead with the bottom of his T-shirt.

'What's the matter, little brother?' Jack asked. 'You getting soft since you left the CIA?'

'Yeah, it's that academic life,' Mike said, grinning.

Andie didn't think his muscles looked soft, so his sabbatical in Japan must have been physically challenging as well as mentally rewarding.

'Aren't you glad to see us, Andie Candy?' Mike teased.

His use of his personal nickname for her made her feel teary-eyed. She was a mess. And she didn't want them to know about it either.

'Of course, I'm glad to see you guys. I'm just tired, and it's hot out here. Let's go inside and catch up.'

Later after they'd all showered, Andie and her brothers went to their favorite burger hangout which featured a nickel jukebox. They played songs that had been oldies when they were all babies. Her brothers each discussed what they'd been working on — or rather they told her as much as they could, given their different security levels.

When Jack casually asked if she'd been dating anyone new lately, she knew their visit home was no accident.

'You guys are something else.' She blushed the way she had at eighteen, when they'd caught her necking with her boyfriend after the prom.

'What?' they chimed in unison.

'This is ridiculous,' Andie sputtered. 'I'm a grown woman. How dare Dad call you and tell you about my . . . my . . . ' She didn't know how to finish that sentence. 'Was it Dad or Grandad?' she finally asked.

'Both,' her brothers answered.

'Well, I'm pleading the fifth. This is none of their business and it's not yours, either.'

'Oh, come on, Andie,' Evan said. 'We're just worried about you.'

'Yeah, it's not like you to come dragging in at sunrise,' Greg said.

Andie blushed hotly.

'Way to go, Greg,' his twin said, punching him on the bicep.

'Oww,' he howled.

'Serves you right, stupid,' said Jack.

'We just want to make sure you're all

right,' Mike said.

'I'm just fine, thank you very much, or I will be if y'all keep your questions to yourself. I don't go around asking about your sex life.'

'Andie!' Jack said, sounding outraged. 'Don't talk like that.'

She laughed at him and her other guardians. 'You guys are too much. Especially with what I know about you and your girlfriends — even back in high school.'

'Hey, it's okay for guys to have a sex life, but sisters are different,' Mike said.

As usual, her brothers didn't give up — they just changed tactics. Each brother found a way to get her alone. Then he tried his best to pry information out of her. Andie refused to divulge anything and somehow managed to sneak away from them while they were all shooting pool upstairs in the game room.

She felt like an idiot having to duck out of her own house, she thought, driving away in her Miata, but she didn't care. Once on the road, she went with a racing heart and expectation that made her throb in places that should have made her feel embarrassed but didn't.

'You're crazy,' she told herself when she parked next to Bruce's truck. She shouldn't be so eager — after all, he'd extorted this promise to meet him — but she practically flew up the stairs to the third floor. The door was open before she knocked.

'What kept you?' he asked, pulling her into his arms. They kissed and kissed. Finally, he seemed to remember the door stood wide open. He shoved it closed with his foot and drew her straight to the bedroom. Andie didn't argue. In fact, she couldn't have said a word if her life had depended on it. Passion swept away all logical thought. All she wanted was to experience the same expression of love as last night.

Minutes later, she had Bruce outstretched in the middle of the bed while she kissed and teased him in a way that drove him wild with need. When he moaned and begged her to stop, she smiled triumphantly. 'You said I could do with you as I wanted.' She reached up to brush a lock of hair from his forehead.

Bruce grabbed her wrists. Before she could blink, he'd shifted positions until he was on top. 'Now it's my turn.' His eyes were hot as he did his best to satisfy her every desire. When he'd succeeded beyond expectations, he whispered, 'Andie?'

She opened her eyes. 'Yes?'

'Say you'll give us a chance.'

Mute, she stared at him as his words dragged her back to reality.

'Say it,' Bruce demanded as he opened her to receive him.

The moment froze in time. Finally, Andie moaned the answer he was looking for, and he plunged inside her. Her moan became a cry at her moment of ultimate fulfillment . . . and Bruce's simultaneous climax.

Later, when they lay together, awake this time, she wondered at the logic of what she'd promised. As if he could read her thoughts, he said, 'It'll be all right, Andie. We're meant for each other. It'll work out.'

An hour later, with his words echoing in her mind, Andie kissed him goodbye.

'Why do you have to go?' he asked.

'I told you. My brothers are all home for a visit. And I don't want to bump into my dad and granddad at daybreak.'

'Well, we'll have to do something about this,' he said, kissing her for the tenth time as they stood at her car. 'I want to wake up with you beside me in the morning.'

Andie wanted that too, and for the first time, she felt optimistic that Bruce was the man for her. Yes, he was a cop, but so was she. She could handle the pressure, she thought.

As she drove away, she didn't notice the four men in the Suburban parked at the opposite end of the lot. The four men noticed her — and her lover, too.

Hell might have no fury like a woman scorned, but it was nothing compared to the fury of four overprotective brothers.

13

By Saturday, everything was in place. The hotel banquet room where the fashion show was to be held was so heavily air-conditioned, Andie half-expected to see icicles hanging from the ceiling vents.

Darcy had set up a silent auction featuring sports memorabilia arranged on tables ringing the huge room. A runway leading from the stage divided the room into two halves. Folding chairs were set up in rows on either side.

After today, her partnership would be over when she and Bruce arrested Pippo Lombardo, Andie thought, adjusting her waiter's tux. The mirror told her she looked like the rest of the wait staff employed by the caterer to serve champagne and trays of hors d'oeuvres at the swanky fashion show and reception. The black wig she wore was a nice touch, she thought, even if it did itch like the devil.

'Where's Bruce?' Darcy asked, fighting a long strand of hair that had slipped from the loose chignon she wore.

'He's in the men's dressing room with Luis and Peyton.' Andie couldn't even say his name without feeling all mushy inside. She wondered if she looked like a woman in love. *In love*. The two words sent a flutter of pleasure and an equally strong flutter of anxiety through her.

'I hope this works the way Bruce promised it would,' Darcy worried, fidgeting now with the notecards which contained her opening address.

'I'm sure it will. Only a few guests have arrived — with the exception of all the male members of my family.'

'Yes, I don't know if I've thanked you yet for getting your dad to help fund the camp.'

'Only about a million times,' Andie

said. 'Relax, Darcy. It's going to be all right. This'll be a huge success. As soon as Lombardo shows, we'll arrest him and get him out of the way. You're going to raise a lot of money today.'

'I'm scared to death,' Darcy confessed.

'Nothing's going to happen,' Andie reassured her again.

'Not about this Lombardo thing,' Darcy said. 'I'm scared that this will be a total fiasco. I want to raise enough money for the basketball camp, but I'm afraid no one will show!'

'It's going to go like clockwork, I keep telling you,' Andie said. 'You know yourself you've sold nearly all the tickets, so just the admission alone will raise some money.'

'I know. I know. I'm just nervous.'

Andie was tempted to tell her that Tom Luft had called in a few favors. Some of the San Antonio Spurs basketball players and their wives planned to attend the show today, as well as donate some time to the youth teams.

One of the other waiters came over. 'Mrs. Whitaker, the photographer you commissioned is here.'

'Tell him I'm in a meeting at the moment. Have him wait in the foyer. I'll be right there as soon as possible to show him where to set up,' Darcy said, not sounding a bit nervous.

The man hurried away with the message.

'I can't believe he actually showed,' Darcy said. 'Is he stupid? Doesn't he know there's a warrant out for him?'

'Hey, never overestimate the intelligence of a crook.' Andie lifted the walkie-talkie and punched the button. 'It's show time!' Excited and thinking about the future Bruce had sworn they'd have together, she didn't wait for acknowledgement.

As Darcy hurried away, Andie picked up the tray of champagne flutes. She carried it up in the air the way the other waiters did and hurried out to the lobby where a dozen or more people — including her brothers, her father, and her grandfather — milled around.

She saw Pippo Lombardo pacing at the end of the room between the Roman columns. He wore an expensive suit — she wondered if it was a Ralph Lauren — and carried a leather camera bag on his shoulder. He hadn't even done anything to disguise his appearance. She was a little disappointed that he was making it so easy.

In back of him was the hallway that led to the hotel lobby. Pippo looked nervous. Bruce, Luis, and Peyton were supposed to prevent him from leaving through the double doors at that end. Other officers were taking up their positions in the corridors outside the other entrances.

'Champagne, gentlemen?' she asked Tom and Nolan Luft. Her dad took a flute, but Nolan frowned and asked, 'Don't you have any beer?'

Andie refrained from smiling. 'I'm sorry, sir, but there's only champagne.' He waved his hand and declined.

'Miss, over here,' her oldest brother Jack called.

Andie headed toward them. They'd been acting weird all day. 'Champagne?'

They each selected a glass and took their time doing it. Impatiently, she started to leave, but each twin grabbed a wrist and held her in place. 'Just a minute,' Mike, the youngest, said.

'I'm working,' she hissed, glancing toward the end of the room where Lombardo seemed to be getting antsier by the minute. Where were Bruce and the guys?

'Isn't your partner supposed to be here?' Jack asked, looking around.

'Yes, but he's working too,' Andie said. She got a prickly feeling under her skin.

'How long have you known this Benton character?' Evan inquired.

'What?' Andie asked, frowning. She saw Chase emerge from the service entrance. With her attention splintered, she watched Chase walk toward them.

Greg chose that moment to ask, 'Are you aware your partner has quite a reputation with women?'

That statement broke through Andie's worry, and she noticed it piqued Chase's interest. He halted and said, 'It's true. Bruce does have quite a rep. I'm Chase Whitaker, Darcy's husband. Bruce is my brother-in-law. He's a pain in the neck, but I guess he's family. What's your business with him?'

'I've got to move on,' Andie said hurriedly. 'This discussion can wait until later.'

'I think we want to talk about it now,' Jack said, 'especially since you're involved with Benton. Everything about him is our business.'

'Oh, no,' Andie groaned, closing her eyes. 'Jack, don't say another word. This isn't any of your business.'

'He can't just toy with our sister and then toss her away the way he does other women,' Mike said hotly.

'Oh, my! You mean — ' Chase broke off. His laugh drew everyone's eyes.

Andie wanted to crawl into a hold and hide.

'You mean,' Chase gasped between laughs, 'you want to ask Bruce what his intentions are?'

'You're damn right,' her four brothers said in unison.

'Miss? Miss, are you ever going to bring us some of that champagne? Or do I have to come get it?' a querulous voice asked.

Andie blushed beet red. 'Yes, ma'am. I'll be right there.'

'You four idiots better be scattered to the four winds by the time I get home tonight,' she said, turning on her heel to leave.

At the other end of the room, Lombardo still paced nervously. Where was Bruce? Worried, Andie gnawed her lip as she carried the tray to the bossy middle-aged woman who'd reprimanded her. Something was terribly wrong. She distributed the rest of the champagne flutes around to the other guests who weren't part of the police action, but she still didn't see Bruce.

Andie went immediately to her brothers. 'Okay, guys, I decided to speak to you again before hell freezes over. I need your help. Something's gone wrong. See that nervous guy near the entrance?'

At their nod, she said, 'Take an exit door and don't let him leave.' They obeyed without questioning her or making any comment.

After they'd passed Lombardo on their way out, she turned to Chase. 'Can you go tell him Darcy got a run in her stocking or something and that's why she hasn't shown up? Ask him to hang loose and she'll be with him in a moment.'

'Sure. No problem.'

'Oh, and Chase? See if you can get him to come farther into the room. Then go to the dressing room and see where the guys are.'

Chase hurried away to do as she'd asked. Andie hurried back to the kitchen. Once out of sight she grabbed up the walkie-talkie. 'Bruce? Bruce?' No answer. Everything was falling apart.

Taking a deep breath, Andie grabbed another tray of champagne and started out. She needed to get near Lombardo. It was the only way she'd have a chance to bring him down.

Chase was talking to him as she reentered the ballroom. Lombardo shook his head vigorously. After a moment, Chase shrugged and walked away. Lombardo must have declined a chance to sit in one of the chairs while he waited. He still hugged the entrance and seemed more anxious than ever.

Tray held high above her head, Andie hoped his attention would be on the champagne flutes, not on her face. She was only a few feet away when Lombardo suddenly stopped pacing. As if in slow motion, his eyes zeroed in on her face.

'You!' he gasped. Then his hands scrambled for his camera bag and opened it. Just then Andie saw Bruce and his two friends come out of the dressing room.

'You bitch,' Lombardo hissed, pulling out a gun that looked like a toy.

Unfortunately, Andie recognized the Saturday night special for what it was — a dangerous weapon in the hands of an unstable man.

'Young lady, why aren't you serving that champagne?'

As if in slow motion, Andie saw the fussy matron walking up to her. Lombardo moved the gun from Andie to the woman.

The minute she saw the pistol, the woman screamed, 'Gun!' Then she did a nosedive to Lombardo's feet.

The photographer jerked the pistol back to Andie, then to Bruce and his friends. Panicked, he pointed the gun at the terrified crowd. Suddenly, his arm steadied. He swung the gun back to Andie and smiled. There was not a hint of amusement in his smile. She felt her skin crawl.

'This is your fault.' Andie threw the tray with all her strength at the same time he fired. It hit his arm and deflected his aim, and she was on him in an instant. One blow and he was out for the count. A woman's scream punctuated the end of her adventure with Lombardo.

'I got him, Bruce,' Andie crowed, flipping him over on his stomach. She pulled the cuffs from her trousers pocket and slapped them on his wrists. 'Bruce?' She jumped up and turned to find her lover.

In the next instant, she was certain her heart had stopped. Bruce lay on the floor, his head cradled in Darcy's lap. Tears streamed down Darcy's face.

'Call 911,' Peyton bellowed.

Andie walked over. Each step seemed as if it took more effort, energy, and will than she possessed. Chase gently removed the tux jacket Bruce wore. Blood darkened the left side of the white pleated shirt front.

'Bruce?' Andie stood there, swaying as her worst fears became reality.

Dimly she heard someone yell, 'Somebody catch her!'

14

Andie cleaned out the few personal items she'd stashed in Luis's desk and tossed them in the small box she'd brought with her. No messy emotions impeded her progress. To have emotions, you had to have a heart. Hers might be pumping blood through her veins, but that was the only use for it. For all the emotion that filled her, she might as well have been made of wood.

'Good working with you again,' Peyton said, patting her shoulder. 'Don't be a stranger.'

She tried to smile. 'Same here, Peyton.' She hugged him, then turned to Luis who was ready to take his desk back. She gave him a sad little smile. 'Thanks for the loan of the desk and your chair, Luis.'

'Anytime, Andie.' Luis cracked his knuckles. 'Uh, Bruce'll be here any minute. Don't you want to wait and see him before you leave?'

Her heart seemed to shrink inside her chest. It hurt so much. She wished there was some way to lessen the pain — although it did prove that her heart wasn't made of wood, after all.

'No. You tell him goodbye for me,' she managed to say without breaking down. Then she picked up the box and walked out without a backward glance, waving casually to the other guys as she pushed the door open.

If luck had been with her, she'd have seen Bruce before he saw her. But it wasn't. He was sitting on the trunk of her car.

'Hi,' he said.

'Hi.'

'Cleaned out your desk, I see.'

'Yes.'

'You were going to just leave without even saying goodbye?'

Her eyes dropped to the coffee mug in the box. *Women cops do it with pantyhose and guns*, it said.

'Well?'

'I thought it best that way.'

'Well, I don't think it's best. If you want to know what I think, I think it's cowardly. I think it sucks.'

'Let's not do this,' she whispered. Her grip on the box tightened until her knuckles were white.

Bruce hopped off the trunk and reached for the box with his right hand, then dropped it into the back of his pickup. He opened the passenger door and said, 'Get in.'

Andie stood, trembling like a leaf in a south Texas breeze. When he reached out and touched her, cupping her cheek gently, a tear splashed from one eye. 'Come on, baby, get in,' he cajoled. He gave her a little push and she walked over to his truck and climbed in. Bruce slammed the door and went around to the driver's side.

Numbly, Andie watched the road, concentrating on holding in the hot tears. She'd spend the afternoon with him. Then she'd end it. It was best for him and for her.

She wasn't surprised when he pulled into his apartment complex. Neither said a word as he took her upstairs. When Bruce sat her down on the sofa, she stirred. With a ghost of a smile, she murmured, 'Aren't we in the wrong room?'

He shook his head as if he didn't trust himself to speak. Then he sat across from her in the leather recliner. Her smile hurt him nearly as much as the groove in the top of his shoulder made by Lombardo's bullet.

'Any room we're in together is the right room,' he said, watching her closely. She refused to meet his eyes. Instead, she rose and came to where he sat and curled into his lap, careful not to put pressure on his left side.

'Andie, we need to talk.'

'I'd rather make love,' she said softly.

With a strained laugh, he said, 'We can do that too, but first we talk.' He sighed. 'I know you're still upset, but it was a freak accident, sweetheart. The important thing is that everything worked out okay. I'm fine.'

'This time,' she said in a sad voice, fiddling with one of his shirt buttons.

He sighed heavily. 'No one can predict the future, Andie. I don't even know what I'm going to have for breakfast tomorrow,' he joked, desperate to break through her fear. 'I wouldn't begin to guess what will happen in the course of my life. Maybe I'll get killed. Maybe you will. We don't know. There are no guarantees in life, but these are the facts as I see them. I'm in love with you. You're in love with me. I want us to get married.'

Her fingers stilled. 'Oh, Bruce,' she said in a voice that held a world of hurt. She kissed his throat, then began to unbutton his shirt. When she had pulled it out from his pants, she began to unbutton her own blouse. Slowly, she opened her shirt and leaned toward him.

'Is that your way of accepting my proposal?'

Andie's eyes popped open. 'Why are you being so difficult?'

'I may be easy, but I'm not free,' he said. With shaking fingers, he slowly rebuttoned her blouse.

'What are you doing?' she asked, sounding as confused as he felt.

Bruce sighed. 'Something I thought I'd never do. I'm refusing your generous offer. If I can't have all of you, I don't want any part of you.'

'What?'

'You heard me.' He pushed her hips. 'Hop off.'

Andie stood, looking down at him as if he were crazy. Hell, he might be, he thought, standing.

'You don't want me?' she asked, sounding as forlorn as he felt.

'Andie, I want you more than any woman I've ever met, but I want more than just sex with you. I want all of you.' He watched her expression change, saw her disbelief crowded out by anger.

'That's blackmail.'

'Yep, it is.'

Andie began to pace. All the fight seemed to go out of her. 'Bruce, it just won't work. When I saw you, wounded, there on the floor . . . '

'I slipped on that spilled champagne, Andie. My hard head denting the floor was what knocked me out — not that little pipsqueak's shot.'

'I know that. Now. Then I thought you were dead. I can't go through that ever again.'

'Andie, you're being foolish.'

'That's easy for you to say. You didn't see my mother crying night after night when my dad was shot. You didn't see her watching the clock, waiting for him to come home. Watching her knuckles turn white when she answered the phone on nights when he was late. I can't go through that.'

'We can go through it together,' he said. 'The same thing could happen to you.'

Andie dismissed his comment with a wave of her hands. 'Just forget me, Bruce. Find someone else.'

'Is that what you intend to do?' he asked, growing angry.

'Yes. Eventually. Maybe. I don't know.'

His lips clamped together. 'I'm not going to beg, Andie. In a week or so when you get over the shock of what happened, you'll regret this decision. You're intelligent — usually. When you start thinking about this, you'll realize you've made a big mistake. Then you're the one who'll have to beg, but I'll make it easy for you, I promise.'

'Just take me back to my car. Please,' she whispered.

★   ★   ★

Five miserable, agonizing days later, Andie had begun to think maybe she had made the biggest mistake of her life.

Two nights after all her brothers had left, her dad said, 'Why don't you go out? It'll do you good to get out of the house.'

'I don't feel like it, Daddy,' she said from the depths of the couch.

Tom Luft sighed and sat on the edge of the couch next to her. 'Honey, you haven't moved from there in days.'

'You're exaggerating.'

'Very little. There's a permanent hollow in the couch cushion.'

'Funny. My dad the comic.'

'Look, Darcy Whitaker called.'

'I know. I don't want to talk to her.' Just thinking about anything or anyone related to Bruce hurt too much to bear.

Tom sighed again. 'She's giving a party to thank everyone who contributed to the youth teams. I can't make it, but I want you to go as a representative for the company.'

'Oh, Daddy, don't ask me to do that.'

'I wouldn't unless it was important. I got some of the Spurs to chip in a big chunk of money. They're going to be there so someone has to go in my place. Come on. It'll be good for you to get out.'

'But I'm on vacation,' she complained.

'Ha. Some vacation. You're practically growing mold.'

'Okay, okay. I'll do it. But I don't have to like it.'

Her attitude about the party hadn't changed by Saturday night as she drove to the Whitakers' house. She'd called Darcy earlier, assured that Bruce would probably not be at the party, Andie thought she'd manage to get through the evening.

About five miles away, Andie pulled out from an intersection as soon as the light changed to green. A purple two-door coupe ran the red light.

Andie saw it from the corner of her eye and stomped the accelerator, trying to get out of its way. Her quick action meant the oncoming driver just missed broadsiding her — but the inevitable collision spun her little red car in a circle. She lost count of how many times it went around, but when it came to rest facing the oncoming traffic, she felt dizzy. She sat there a moment to get her bearings, then took a deep breath and said a quick prayer of thanks.

Grabbing her purse, she climbed out of the car. The teenage girl who'd run the red light was losing her dinner onto the pavement . . . and her car was in much worse shape than Andie's.

'Are you all right?' Andie asked, pulling her cell phone from her purse.

The girl nodded. Andie handed her a tissue to wipe her mouth, then dialed 911. After checking the girl again, she walked back and began directing traffic around the two crumpled vehicles.

Of all endings to an evening she'd dreaded, she'd never have imagined this one. Now she could go home. Even her dad couldn't fault her for not continuing on to the party. She wouldn't have to risk seeing Bruce after all.

In the process of waving a vehicle through the intersection, Bruce's words suddenly came to her.

Maybe I'll get killed. Maybe you will. There are no guarantees.

Despite all her mother's fears and worries, it wasn't her dad who'd died before his time. It was her mother on a routine drive home. Tonight it could have been her.

After the patrol cop showed up to write the accident report and take care of the traffic problem, Andie sat in her car, thinking things over.

Love made you vulnerable. It made you fear for the one you loved, but perhaps that wasn't too high a price to pay. Maybe her mother had difficulty handling the pressure, but she'd never left her father. Andie realized her mother had loved him too much.

A mix of emotions hit Andie hard — shame that she'd been afraid to take the chance of a lifetime — and regret. For the first time since Bruce had been shot, Andie felt as if she were waking up from a dream. What if it was too late?

No! She refused to believe she'd lost the man she loved.

An hour later tow trucks had hauled off both cars. The girl didn't seem to be hurt, so Andie had called her parents who had arrived to take her home. They'd been scolding her about her habit of racing through intersections on the yellow caution light, evidently. Andie sincerely hoped the girl had learned her lesson.

When the patrol cop who'd written the report asked if she needed a ride, Andie grinned and thanked him for the professional courtesy. 'Actually, I was on my way to a friend's home just a few miles from here.'

He agreed to drop her and they got into his patrol car.

All the way there, Andie planned what she'd say to Darcy to enlist her help in getting Bruce to see her. She didn't want to take any chances this time.

'Thanks a lot,' she told the cop as he dropped her in the Whitakers' driveway. Rock music from the B-52s could be heard coming from the backyard. She hummed along to 'Love Shack,' feeling more cheerful than she'd felt in days.

'Sounds like a great party. Tell them

to keep it down,' the patrolman added with a grin.

'Sure thing.' She waved goodbye, then walked to the front door. It was unlocked and she didn't bother ringing the bell but let herself in.

Dim lights burned in the living room. She followed the sound out to the kitchen. The long granite counters there were laden with several kinds of vegetable platters and dip, a couple of watermelons carved into baskets and filled with three kinds of melon balls, platters of sliced roast, barbecue ribs, and fried chicken. There was so much food. For the first time in a week, Andie felt hungry.

She opened one of the pairs of patio doors and stepped out. The noise level back here was nearly deafening. Floating candles decorated the huge diving pool, tiny white lights outlined every tree in the yard, and candle lanterns on the many round tables scattered about the patio and yard created a festive atmosphere. Andie smiled and went in search of her hosts.

Her heart nearly stopped when she saw Bruce stretched out in one of the many chaise longues lining the pool deck. Had Darcy lied to her? It didn't matter. He was here. Smiling happily, she headed toward him. Just then a woman walked up, leaned over and kissed him on the forehead. Andie halted in midstep.

Bruce swung his legs to the side and stood to greet — Andie gasped — the red-headed weather girl from television. So they were back together. The man didn't waste any time. She turned hurriedly, not wanting him to see her. Stumbling and bumping into people, she finally found the patio door into the house.

When she staggered into the kitchen, Darcy and Chase were there. Chase had his wife cornered, a hand braced on either side of where she perched on the countertop. She was laughing and giggling as he nuzzled her neck.

'Andie! You finally got here,' Darcy called out.

Chase turned. 'Hey, Andie. Excuse me while I neck with my wife.'

Darcy punched his bicep. 'Never mind him.'

'Sorry. Excuse me,' Andie stuttered. 'I just dropped in for a minute. I need to be going now.' She walked straight through to the front door. Her hand was on the latch when she realized she didn't have a car.

'Hey, not so fast,' Darcy said, coming up behind her.

Andie sagged against the door. 'Darcy,' she said in a low voice. 'Can you call me a taxi?'

'Well, sure, but — ' She broke off. 'Are you all right, Andie?'

Andie turned. Whatever Darcy saw in her face made her shout for her husband.

The next thing Andie knew she was sitting on their couch with her head between her knees.

'There,' Darcy said, sounding satisfied. 'You've finally got some color back in your face.'

'This is ridiculous,' Andie said,

coming up for air and feeling like a complete fool. 'Being in love isn't supposed to make you swoon like some nineteenth-century virgin, is it?'

Darcy looked amused. 'Well, I don't know. Just who are you in love with?'

'As if you didn't know.'

'It's about time you came to your senses,' Bruce drawled.

Andie blanched as she saw him leaning in the doorway. 'Come to gloat?'

'No, I heard you were about to do another swan dive for the carpet. Since I missed the first one, I thought I'd catch the encore.'

Andie stared at him as he leaned in the doorway. She hadn't seen him in a week. He looked even better than she'd remembered, she thought, knowing she was completely and hopelessly lost. But she'd waited too long. He'd moved on. Just like she'd told him to.

'At least you didn't bring that brainless bimbo to watch,' she muttered.

'What brainless bimbo would that be?' Bruce asked, walking over to crouch on the floor next to where she sat.

Andie flushed. 'Sorry. I shouldn't be a sore loser. I'm sure your weather girl is very — very — ' She stopped, unable to finish the lie.

'Nice?' he suggested, a look of amusement in his beautiful eyes.

Andie nodded. 'Yes. Nice. Well, it's been, um, nice seeing you again, but if you'll excuse me, I think I'll be going now.'

She started to rise, but Darcy pushed her down with a hand to her shoulder. 'You said you needed a cab. Remember?'

'Oh, yeah. I forgot.'

'Where's your Miata?'

Andie shrugged. 'In the car hospital, I guess — at least the waiting room. I had a little accident on the way over.'

'What?' Bruce leaned close, studying her eyes as if looking for signs of concussion or injury.

'I'm fine. Really. I didn't mean to disrupt the party. Go on back to your . . . your . . . ' She trailed off.

'You don't sound fine.' He turned to his sister. 'Why don't you and Chase go get her some ice water.'

After they'd left the room, Bruce said, 'Are you sure you want to send me into the arms of another woman?'

'What are you talking about? You're already in her arms. And you didn't wait a minute, either!'

Just then the woman in question sauntered into the living room. A man nearly two feet taller trailed after her.

'Bruce, it was nice seeing you again,' the weather girl said, taking the arm of the man Andie recognized as one of the San Antonio Spurs.

'You too, Monica. Take care.' They nodded to Andie and then left.

Bruce turned back to Andie. 'You were saying?'

Andie opened her mouth but nothing came out. She looked at Bruce. Finally she said, 'I'm confused.'

'That's obvious.'

'I thought . . . I saw her kiss you outside.'

'But you didn't see me kiss her back, did you?'

Andie felt a flicker of hope in her heart. 'No, I didn't.'

'Why do you think that is?'

The tiny flicker burst into full flame. 'Because you love me?'

'Maybe.'

She frowned. 'What do you mean maybe?'

'Remember what I said?'

Andie fell silent. Contrite, she said, 'You mean when you told me I'd have to beg?'

Bruce nodded. He moved to sit on the couch next to her, crossed his legs, clasped his hands behind his head and leaned back nonchalantly. 'Go ahead. I'm ready.'

Andie burst into delighted laughter. When she caught her breath, he hadn't moved. 'I'm still waiting.'

She rose and stepped close to him,

then without warning, she climbed onto his lap, straddling him.

'Oomph,' he said. 'You gain weight in the last week?'

'Watch it, Benton,' Andie said, gripping his shirt front in her hands. 'Don't push it.'

'Yes, ma'am, Sergeant, ma'am.'

She took his face in both her hands and said, seriously, with no signs of joking, 'Sergeant Benton?'

'Yes, Sergeant Luft?' He grinned.

'It's been brought to my attention very recently that there are no guarantees in life. I might get hit by a car.'

His grin faded.

'A meteorite might fall through the roof and flatten us both ten minutes from now.'

'Sounds painful.'

'What would be even more painful is to go through life without you.'

'I see. Is there something you're trying to say?'

Andie took a deep breath and kissed him on the lips. 'I'm trying to say I love you. You love me. We can take care of each other and take whatever comes together.'

Bruce arched a dark brow. 'Isn't there some question you want to ask me?'

Andie rolled her eyes. 'You're really going to make me ask this time, aren't you?'

'Fair's fair.' He smiled. His hand rose to trace her lips. 'I told you you'd have to work for it.'

'Oh, for heaven's sake! All right. Will you — '

'Marry me?' he broke in. 'I also told you I'd help you out.'

Andie laughed and kissed him again. This time he deepened the kiss until they were both breathless.

'So what's your answer?' she asked.

'Let me think about it,' he said.

'You rat!' Andie shoved her fingers through his hair and tugged.

'Ouch! Just kidding. Just kidding,' he said, laughing as he pulled her to him again.

Epilogue

'Pssst, Bruce!' Chase Whitaker whispered. 'Come here, quick.'

'What's going on?' Bruce asked, walking out into the hall from the groom's dressing room.

'Darcy's got Andie pinned down in the bride's changing room. Hurry!'

'What do you mean?' Bruce asked as he jogged down the hall beside his brother-in-law. Darcy stood outside the door to the bride's dressing room with the bridesmaids gathered around her.

'Good luck,' Darcy said. She squeezed his shoulder and opened the door.

Bruce crept in. Andie was dressed, but her veil was flipped backward so he could see her lovely face. She sat in a chair in front of a lighted mirror. He walked up behind her. She saw his reflection. Their eyes met. Instantly, he saw the panic that filled her eyes.

His hands cupped her shoulders and squeezed. 'You look incredible.'

'Thank you,' she said, so softly he had to strain to hear.

'It'll all be over in minutes,' he reassured her. Again, he wished he'd carted her off to a justice of the peace the day after their mutual proposal. As the weeks had passed leading up to their big day, her nervousness and anxiety had increased.

'I know. I'm okay. Really. I'm just — '

'Terrified?' Bruce grinned. 'And they say men get nervous. I'm as cool as a cucumber. You, Luft, are shaking like a leaf.'

Andie didn't answer. He leaned close. 'You know I have a pair of handcuffs with me. I brought them just in case.'

'You wouldn't!'

'Hey, never underestimate a desperate man.' He felt the tenseness begin to leave her shoulders.

'Are you a desperate man?'

'Incredibly desperate to be your

husband. So move your fanny, Luft. Let's get this show on the road.'

Andie took a deep breath and stood. She looked elegant and regal, but her voice was pure steel. 'Don't tell me what to do, Benton. Just because I'm marrying you doesn't mean you can order me around.'

'No?' He pulled her into his arms. He wanted to kiss her, but he didn't want to smear her carefully applied lipstick.

'Well, maybe you can . . . ' Andie said suddenly. She kissed him with passion, forgetting all about her makeup. Then she added, 'When it's something I want to do, that is.'

Bruce laughed. 'I'll remember that.'

'See that you do,' Andie said. 'Forget the handcuffs. I'll come peacefully. Let's go get married.'

We do hope that you have enjoyed reading this large print book.

Did you know that all of our titles are available for purchase?

We publish a wide range of high quality large print books including:
Romances, Mysteries, Classics
General Fiction
Non Fiction and Westerns

Special interest titles available in large print are:
The Little Oxford Dictionary
Music Book, Song Book
Hymn Book, Service Book

Also available from us courtesy of Oxford University Press:
Young Readers' Dictionary
(large print edition)
Young Readers' Thesaurus
(large print edition)

For further information or a free brochure, please contact us at:
Ulverscroft Large Print Books Ltd.,
The Green, Bradgate Road, Anstey,
Leicester, LE7 7FU, England.
Tel: (00 44) **0116 236 4325**
Fax: (00 44) **0116 234 0205**

LOVE WILL FIND A WAY

Joan Reeves

Texan Darcy Benton would give anything to be the kind of woman who could captivate her new boss Chase Whitaker. However, the sexy CEO would hardly fall for someone like Darcy, with her straight-laced office wardrobe. Enter Darcy's matchmaking pal, Janet. She transforms her into a bombshell worthy of Chase's undying devotion. Darcy is soon letting her hair down and swapping her boxy suits for slinky dresses. And as Chase becomes intrigued — he's ready for anything . . . including true love.

PICTURES OF THE PAST

Jean M. Long

Lydia's Aunt Mattie goes on a cruise with her friend Joel, and asks Lydia to run her guesthouse near Ullswater. But Joel's nephew Luke Carstairs is also there to help, and Lydia resents his interference. She also resents his interest in her family history, and his reticence to talk about his own background. And what is the mystery about the old photograph album? How can Lydia find the truth, and cope with her growing attraction to Luke?